LOVE, LAUGHTER AND HAPPILY EVER AFTER

A SHORT STORY COLLECTION

DAISY PRESCOTT

COPYRIGHT

Take Two Copyright © Daisy Prescott 2014, All rights reserved.

Take for Granted © Daisy Prescott 2015, All rights reserved.

Outdoor Shower © Daisy Prescott 2017, All rights reserved.

Take the Cake and Run © Daisy Prescott 2014, All rights reserved.

Take it Easy © Daisy Prescott 2015, All rights reserved.

Give and Take © Daisy Prescott 2015, All rights reserved.

Two Wingmen and a Baby © Daisy Prescott 2016, All rights reserved.

Olaf's Christmas Carol © Daisy Prescott 2016, All rights reserved.

The Pink Pearl © Daisy Prescott 2013, All rights reserved.

A NOTE FROM DAISY

Thank you for picking up this collection of short stories from my Modern Love Stories and Wingmen series.

Over the years I've received hundreds of messages and emails asking if I'll write more of certain characters. While each love story is complete with a HEA, the characters continue to live on in my mind and for the readers who love them. It's tough to say good-bye to our book boyfriends and fictional friends when a book ends. A peek into the future is always fun for me to write and wonderful to share with you.

Several of the stories have hidden Easter Eggs for other novels if you're paying attention. Can you spot them?

I hope you enjoy spending time again with your favorite characters from my series.

Thanks for reading!

xo Daisy

Make sure you're subscribed to my monthly emails. I share exclusive shorts, sneak peeks, excerpts, and all my latest news directly to your inbox. I promise never to spam you. You can subscribe at www.daisyprescott.com/newsletter/

TAKE TWO

A MODERN LOVE STORY SHORT

INTRODUCTION

Take Two was included in the first volume of the LOL Anthology and is my first story to hit the USA Today Best Sellers' list. Four years after publication, readers still ask about the characters from *Geoducks Are for Lovers.* I love hearing readers are Team Gil. This short is a glimpse into their lives a few months after their college reunion and overlaps with the beginning of *Ready to Fall.* I love interweaving the Modern Love Story characters with my Wingmen.

Life rarely gives second chances.

With the help of meddling friends, the world's largest burrowing clam, and a hot lumberjack, Maggie Marrion and Gil Morrow got their second chance at love in *Geoducks Are for Lovers.*

Now living together, they're discovering that sometimes the second time around, especially when it comes to sex, is better than the first. Or can be with the help of magical blue pills.

Is a trip to the ER worth it for a night of wild sex at forty?

Take Two is intended for mature audiences, 18 and up, because it contains middle age people kissing, recreational prescription drug use, and outdated references to the late 20th century.

This *Modern Love Story Short* takes place chronologically after Geoducks Are for Lovers and before Wanderlust.

CHAPTER 1

MAGGIE

*riday ...*

Cardboard boxes and plastic bins cluttered the downstairs of Gil's house. I'd been spending more and more time here since the reunion. Last weekend, we'd finally gone to the island and loaded two cars full of boxes, which contained more kitchen stuff than clothes. Or shoes. Luckily, Gil had bachelor cupboards and closets. I teased him about his limited collection of mismatched bowls, pint glasses and single cookie sheet, but I was delighted for all the extra space.

His constant reminders that his house was now our house made me happy in a way I'd never imagined six months ago. My beloved stainless steel stand mixer sat on the counter next to his deluxe coffee/espresso machine.

"Why does anyone need so many glass jars?" he asked, emptying one of my boxes, glass clinking against glass.

"Why does anyone need so many pint glasses?" I gestured at the open cabinet.

"Beer, water, gin & tonics … iced tea." He smiled. "Want me to go on?"

"You've covered four of the major beverage groups."

"I have wine glasses, too."

"It looks like you've done all your shopping in the gift shops of micro-breweries and wineries."

"And that's a bad thing?" His chuckle was low and settled deep under my skin.

"Not at all." I set my Mason jars alongside his collection on the shelf.

"Are you smiling at the cupboard?" He stood behind me and wrapped his arms around my waist.

I tried and failed to temper my grin. "I am. I'm remembering the first time we shared a kitchen." I wondered if we'd still dance to "Call Me Al" in this kitchen the way we had all those years ago.

"Listen Betty, college didn't count." Gil's chest rumbled with his laughter against my back. He'd remembered too. "Plus, we had housemates."

"We were friends."

"Without benefits." He swept my hair down my back.

"We were friends."

"We were silly youth who thought we knew everything and had all the time in the world to let things unfold." He kissed the top of my head.

"Silly, stupid girl." I couldn't argue with him. My smile returned thinking about this moment and this life, and how unexpected and right it felt to be here.

"It's ridiculous how happy I am right now." I pulled his hand to my lips and kissed the back.

"Happy enough for pie making?"

"Is this a euphemism or real pie, involving filling?"

His arms tightened around me and he dragged his scruff over the skin between the collar of my sweater and my jaw. I shivered.

Oh, two could play at this game. I arched my back and rubbed my ass against his jeans.

"Filling could apply to either." His fingers slid closer to my breasts. "I love your pie. What kind is up to you."

"Filling? Really?"

"You said it first."

My heart thumped quicker in my chest. After months of flirting on the phone, our not-so-dirty euphemisms still made me smile. They weren't sexy, or really all that dirty, but they were goofy like us. "I'll never get all these boxes unpacked."

"Let's chuck them all. We can live with pint glasses, jars and paper plates." His hands traveled over the soft swell of my bra and he stepped impossibly closer. He lowered his voice. "I'd rather fill a box—"

"Gil…"

"Maggie…" He squeezed me while grinding his hips.

"You're kidding about the paper plates, right?"

His chuckle was muffled, but audible. "I'm trying seduce you and get you to make out with me. Forget about the unpacking."

"Oh," I said when his fingers found my nipples.

"Oh," he said. "I do believe she's catching on now."

"The unpacking can wait."

"It can."

I peered over my shoulder into his deep brown eyes. "We could at least clear off the counter."

He glanced behind us at the island and then quickly back at me with a silent question.

"It looks like it could be an ideal height."

His expression morphed with restrained excitement. "For?"

"Rolling out pie crust." I turned in his arms to face him and pushed against his chest, encouraging him to back up.

He groaned and grabbed my ass, pulling me along with him. "I'm sure it'll be great for that, but let's test it out for other things first." He grinned, and then swept his arm out, knocking the empty boxes to the floor where they landed with soft thuds.

I matched his expression. Dark hair surrounded a face I'd known half my life. I trailed my hands over the deep green thermal covering his broad shoulders and down his toned biceps.

His long fingers wrapped around my waist and easily lifted me up to the cool granite of the counter. He settled his hips between my legs before kissing me softly at the corner of my mouth.

"Nothing more than this," he whispered against my ear, his warm breath tickling me as he sang along to the song playing on the kitchen's speakers.

I hummed at his words and the memories they conjured. My gaze met his for a few beats.

This man. This man was everything.

I reached for his fly and what strained hard and heavy beneath the denim.

Our pants ended up on the floor as we lost ourselves in each other. Hands swept over warm skin. Tongues teased and tasted. I tugged down his boxers until they skimmed his legs to puddle at his feet. I was right. This counter was the perfect height for his six foot frame.

I opened my mouth to speak, only to be interrupted by the electric chime of the doorbell.

"Expecting anyone?" he asked, his breath husky from our counter encounter.

"No one ever expects the kraken."

"We're landlocked."

"Land shark?" I asked.

He responded by tugging on my earlobe with his teeth.

I moaned. "There's a river. Two rivers. Double the odds for a kraken."

"Do krakens live in the Willamette?"

"I was thinking more the Columbia."

"Oh, sure, the Columbia. Don't they need the deep, dank depths of the oceans?" He pulled away to meet my gaze.

"You're questioning kraken habitat?"

"No, of course not. That would be silly."

The ringing from the hall continued.

"Should we get that?" I asked.

"Probably."

"We could pretend we're not home."

Loud knocking replaced the chimes of the doorbell.

"They seem pushy for Jehovah's Witnesses. Or those sweet Mormon missionary boys."

He raised an eyebrow. "Do you have a thing for young men on bicycles?"

I laughed. "No, but my grandmother used to invite them in for lemonade and cookies. Then, flirted with them."

A combination of knocking and ringing created a cacophony at the front door.

Gil sighed and reached for his jeans. "I should probably put my pants back on and answer it."

"Go pants-less. That'll show them."

He shuffled himself back into his boxers and jeans. I watched his long fingers button his fly, mourning the loss of the view.

"That looks uncomfortable." I pointed at the outline of his hard length.

"It's not ideal." He shook his head.

"It's a shame really." I pouted. "Damn kraken."

"You might want to get dressed in case it's someone we know," he called out as he walked down the hall. "I'm coming."

"You were about to." I snickered.

"Get dressed, Maggie May. It's Selah."

At the mention of my best friend's name, I hopped off the counter, straightened my sweater, and then located my jeans on the floor near the stove.

"What's this about coming?" Selah's voice rang out from the door.

I hopped around, pulling up my jeans as her boots echoed down the hall.

"Damn it, I knew I shouldn't have brought up the kraken three times. Selah's like Beetlejuice." I smiled when her familiar dark bob appeared at the entrance to the kitchen.

"Who are you calling a kraken?" Selah eyed my disheveled appearance, scanning my rumpled clothing. "You might want to zip your jeans, Maggie. Looks like I'm interrupting something delightful." Glee danced in her green eyes.

I quickly adjusted and zipped my jeans. "As a matter of fact—"

"Maggie was about to make a pie." Gil interrupted.

Selah's head turned as she studied the kitchen. A few full boxes sat on the counter and empty boxes lay on their sides, scattered across the floor. There was no flour, or other baking supplies, in sight. She returned her focus to me and arched her eyebrow. "Really? We're going with the pie euphemism?"

My cheeks heated.

"Well, that blush, and the fact you can still blush at your advanced age, tells me everything I need to know." She patted my hair, which was tangled from Gil's fingers.

After swatting away her hands and then smoothing down my hair, I opened the fridge to cool my face, mumbling about krakens and Beetlejuice. "Want something to drink?"

"No, can't stay. Just stopping by to drop off your house-warming gift."

"I've lived here for years," Gil said.

"You don't count. Okay, it's more of a shacking up gift."

"Please don't let it be a sex swing or restraints, or other kinky stuff," I said mostly to myself.

"As if I'd buy you two a sex swing." She looked up to the ceiling. "I'm not sure these plaster ceilings could handle it."

"I don't know whether or not to be insulted," Gil said.

"Oh, I know the best place to get one if you want me to take this back." She placed a red gift bag on the counter.

"You have a sex swing?" My voice revealed both my fear and fascination about her answer.

"No, not me. Whatshisface from the tech startup did. You know all those successful businessmen, captain of industry types, are into the kinky stuff." Her sigh held an unspoken nostalgia.

"Before this turns into Cougar Confessions, are you sure you don't want a beer or wine? Coffee?" Gil walked over to my newly organized cupboard and grabbed a pint glass. He held it up and smiled at me.

I rolled my eyes.

"Okay, fine. Twist my arm. I'll have coffee." Selah settled herself on one of the counter stools.

While the scent of brewing coffee filled the kitchen, Gil and Selah chatted about their upcoming classes and who had the worse teaching load for spring semester.

"What's happening with your beach cabin while you two play love nest down here in Portland?" she asked, adding cream to her cup.

"I was going to leave it empty for the winter, but Quinn called from New York asking for a favor. A friend of his and Ryan's needs a short term rental. Bad divorce. How could I say no?" When Quinn called and explained about his friend Diane's bastard soon-to-be-ex-husband, I couldn't turn her away. Divorce was tough enough when it was amicable or apathetic. I knew from experience.

"Is she hot?" Selah asked.

"Are you asking for yourself?"

She scoffed. "No, for John. I'm sure he misses flirting with you every day."

Gil grumbled from his corner of the counter.

"I hadn't even thought about John. The whole thing happened so quickly. Guess I should let him know."

"I'd hate for John to show up for his morning Maggie—sorry Gil, I mean coffee—and be devastated." Selah smiled with her typical twinkle in her eye. The finger twirling a short lock of her hair was the tell that she was up to no good and deliberately pushing Gils buttons.

Gil growled and muttered, "I'm sure the lumberjack will be fine on his own."

"Does the caveman thing turn you on, Maggie?" Selah laughed. "Cause it's working for me. I didn't know if you had it in you, G."

"Works for me, too." I winked at her and wrapped my arms around his hips. He leaned down to kiss me softly on the lips. I kissed him back for a moment, rekindling what Selah had interrupted.

"Gah, you two are like horny teenagers." She coughed.

I smiled up at the man I loved. His hair had silver sprinkled through the dark, but his eyes were the same ones that made me swoon in college.

"Okay, before you two start making out again, or finish whatever it was you were doing when I arrived." She eyed the counter and strewn boxes. "Open your gift."

I carefully lifted the bag and peered inside.

Gil leaned over my shoulder and whispered, "Why do I feel a little nervous?"

"Because it's Selah?" I asked.

"Stop it. Open my gift, you lovebirds." She huffed.

I reached inside the bag and pulled out a small blue and white box.

Gil inhaled behind me and stiffened, but not in the good way. "This better be a joke."

"Now, now, no one is questioning your manhood. I just thought it would be fun for you two. You know, recreationally. I got them from that doctor I was seeing, so they're legit. You can role-play horny teenagers. Or horny college students I should say. Second chances and all that."

I could feel my whole neck and face heat. I touched the tip of my ears as if I could feel their pink color.

"Selah—"

"Maggie—" She echoed me. "Quit glaring at me, Gil. Come on, it's a gag gift!"

I snorted. "Nice pun."

She preened. "I'm pretty proud of that one."

I stuffed the box back inside the bag and out of sight.

"You haven't even found the real gift yet." She pouted.

"I don't think Gil can handle any more presents right now. I'm sure we'll love it no matter what you got us."

"Unless it's a penis pump. Then you're banned from the house." Gil smiled, but crossed his arms and glowered at her. "I'm serious."

"Okay, okay." She held up her hands. "I'm done with my coffee and have a million errands today. Dinner later in the week, Magpie?"

"Sure." I kissed her cheek before she walked down the hall.

Halfway between the kitchen and foyer, she called out, "Watch out for priapism!" With that she scampered out the door, her laughter lingering behind her.

"Why are we still friends with her?"

"Because we love her, and without her, I probably wouldn't be here in your kitchen."

"Our kitchen." He reminded me before kissing me again, snaking his hands under my sweater, and pulling me close.

We broke apart a few moments later, both of us breathing a little faster than before.

"We should straighten up this mess." I glowered at the chaos in the kitchen.

"Leave it. Let's go to dinner." He dug through the gift bag again, and pulled out the little box.

"What are you doing with that? I thought you were pissed at Selah."

He shrugged.

A smile tugged at my lips. "Someone's curious." It wasn't a question and I couldn't hide my amusement or own curiosity. He didn't need help, but well, he wasn't eighteen anymore either.

"Sounds like I'm not the only one." He arched an eyebrow.

I sucked in my cheeks and let my gaze flit around the ceiling. Damn. I was curious. Nothing to complain about in our brief sex life, but my inner twenty-something did wonder what she'd missed all those years we'd been apart.

'You are so curious, Maggie May. Your face says it all."

"All right, all right. I am. But not tonight. I'm tired and smelly from unpacking. Rain check?" I looked down at my hands stained with newsprint from the paper wrapped around the glasses.

He kissed the tip of my nose. "Deal."

CHAPTER 2

GIL

The next afternoon, Maggie's laughter carried down the hall into my office, breaking me out of the trance of finalizing my sophomore history class reading list.

I found her standing in my bedroom at the foot of the unmade bed. Our bedroom. Her eyes sparkled with amusement.

"Is that a Star Wars pillowcase?" she asked.

"It might be, yes." I glanced at the bed, our bed, where the pillowcase in question sat on a stack of folded sheets.

She grinned at me. "How does a grown man come to have a Star Wars pillowcase in his possession?"

"Don't be dissing on the vintage Star Wars collectible memorabilia." I picked up the pillowcase and unfolded it, before running my hand over the familiar faces.

"Did you just pet a pillowcase?"

I nodded. "I've had it forever."

"You mean, from when the movies first came out?" Her voice carried an incredulous note.

I nodded again. "Yep."

"Gilliam Morrow, you are a sentimental fool."

My smile matched hers. "Damn straight."

"Only one?"

"Twin bed."

She raised her eyebrows and her lips formed a small "o" shape. Her eyes softened.

I knew that look. I picked up a pillow and gently whacked her shoulder.

"You're imagining me in that bed, aren't you?"

The pink darkening on her cheeks answered my question. "Not in a perverted way. You were a kid."

"Your cheeks say something different, sweetheart."

She shook her head and her golden red waves settled over her shoulders.

"Okay, okay. I admit the thought of young Gil makes my heart swoon."

"Young or younger?"

"Well, not the one who slept on this pillowcase."

"I still had it in college. Don't you remember?"

I watched as her forehead scrunched up in thought. "You did?"

"Freshman year. Until Ben called me a nerd and told me I'd never get laid."

"Ben would say that." She laughed. "So you ditched the force?"

"I did."

"How'd that work out for you and the getting laid?"

"Pretty well." I met her eyes and our shared history flickered behind her lashes. "Although, from your expression, I'm thinking I should have kept on being a nerd."

"Why's that?" She stepped around the bed, moving to stand by my side. She tilted her head to peer up at me.

"Maybe I would have got the girl instead." I leaned down to brush my lips against hers.

"You got me now," she whispered against my mouth. "I'll have sex with you, silly pillowcase and all."

"Silly?" I stepped back to stare down at her. "Silly? The greatest film franchise ever, in the history of film franchises, and you call it silly?"

A familiar spark returned to her eye. She was teasing, pushing my buttons. "Two words—"

"Don't say Jar Jar." I scowled.

"I was going to say "gold bikini." She shrugged. "Isn't that every man's fantasy?"

I swallowed heavily. She was right. Most men of a certain age had a fantasy at one time or another about Leia's skimpy outfit and Phoebe Cate's red bikini.

"You so did. I can see the lust all over your face." She teased.

I gave her a wolfish grin. "I'm imagining you in that bikini now."

"You want to role play? You can be Jabba"

She squealed when I picked her up and threw her on the bed, toppling the stack of sheets and pillowcases onto the floor.

"I should keep you tied to this bed."

Her eyes slowly blinked up at me, her chest heaving with her surprise and laughter. "Okay," she whispered.

"Okay what?" I dragged my nose along her jawline.

"You can use the pillowcase."

"So that's a no on the gold bikini?"

She nodded.

"And the tied to the bed part?"

"Negotiable." A slow smile teased her lips.

I arched an eyebrow at her. "Oh, really?"

She responded by pulling my head down, melting her mouth with mine. When she opened, I responded by sweeping my tongue against hers. Our kiss found a rhythm we first discovered decades ago, simultaneously familiar and new. I grasped her neck, angling her head to devour her. Lost in her taste, my feet slipped on the floor, and I fell heavily on top of her.

"Oomph."

"Sorry." I adjusted myself to brace my weight on my hips and elbow.

After a few minutes of kissing and rounding second base, she asked, "So, thoughts about Selah's gift?"

I smiled against her shoulder and bit her skin with enough pressure to make her yelp. "Why do you ask?"

"Well ..."

I waited for her to explain and occupied myself with unbuttoning her shirt. She squirmed under my touch.

"I was thinking we could have a do-over with that fantasy of yours."

"You have a gold bikini?"

"No, the getting laid in college." She paused and I could see the meaning of her words clicking into place in her mind. "Not that you didn't get laid in college. I meant with me. On that pillowcase."

"And that has to do with the magical pills how?"

"The two might complement each other." She sat up and shrugged, not meeting my eyes.

"Maggie?"

"Hmmm."

"Look at me."

Her gaze swept over my face before meeting my eyes. "I'd like nothing more than to fuck you silly like I should have freshman year, if I'd had the courage."

I watched her pupils dilate and her breath pause for a moment until she let out a slow, quiet exhale.

"You're on, Morrow." She untangled her legs from mine and crawled over me to get to her nightstand.

Sneaky woman had tucked the box away already.

"Are you sure?" she asked, her voice hesitant.

"Yeah. It's kind of like the *Matrix*."

"I remember when you made that reference last summer."

I remembered, too. We were at a crossroads of living in memories of the past or choosing to create new ones together.

"In this case, the blue pill is the better choice." She held out the pills.

"I'll take it if you want."

"Only if you want to. No pressure from me." Maggie looked down at the blue tablets still safely ensconced in their silvery packet.

"I could be up for it." I smiled at her.

"Pun intended?"

"What's the worst that can happen?" I brushed my hand along her cheek.

"A never-ending erection? A trip to the ER and the embarrassment of having to tell a doctor what's wrong with you?"

"If that happens, you have to promise never to breath a word of it to anyone."

"So you're willing to risk all that for a roll in the hay?" Amusement colored her question.

"Sure, as long as no actual hay is involved."

"Okay, bottoms up!" She handed me the glass of water from my nightstand.

"Pun intended?" I knew my sly smile matched the devilish glint in my eyes. I also knew she wasn't really suggesting backdoor action.

"No." She rolled her eyes.

"No to the pun or the deed?"

"No to the pun. Negotiable on the deed."

"Oh, really?" My eyebrows felt like they were trying to escape from the top of my head.

"At a later date."

"Well, then. Nothing to do but engage in illegal prescription drug use." I eyed the packet.

She giggled. "I'm nervous. I don't know why. It's not like it will be different. I mean the equipment is the same and all. We've had sex before. A lot of sex. Not random and infrequent encounters, but consistent, sometimes daily, sometimes multiple orgasms in a night—"

I stopped her. "You're babbling."

"I am. And you're not opening the packet."

I stalled for time. "What's the most orgasms you've had in a day?"

"Alone? Or with someone?" Her expression gave nothing away.

"For the sake of the current discussion, let's limit it to with a partner."

She twisted her lips in thought. "Three? Four? There was that weekend after Olympia ..."

I remembered that weekend. Knowing I was the one to hit her record, I felt my confidence return. "Let's see if we can double that number."

"Oh," she whispered.

I looked down before pressing the edge of my thumbnail into the foil. "Should I put on the Cocteau Twins to set the mood?"

Her laughter answered me. "No, not needed. Come here," she asked as she fell back against the bed.

I swallowed the pill. "How long do we wait?"

"I have no idea. It's your penis. Won't you feel something down there?"

"I'm already feeling something from a few minutes ago." I did that move that teenage boys do—I reached for her hand and placed it on the bulge in my jeans.

"Wow, that worked quick." She teased, tracing the visible bulge.

"Maybe this was a mistake." I lay next to her again, staring at the ceiling, waiting for something to feel different. Her knuckle ran down the length of my cock. Okay, it didn't feel different, but it did feel good.

"Only one way to find out." Kneeling between my legs, she unzipped my pants and reached into the fly.

"What if it doesn't ever go down?" A creeping worry infiltrated my brain. "Should we note the time?" I tried to sit up to see my alarm clock. Her hand pushed me back on the bed.

Speaking of going down, Maggie's head moved south until her warm breath tickled my happy trail. "Relax."

How could I relax when her head was there and the wet heat of her mouth teased me? I clenched the pillows above my head when her mouth engulfed me.

I knew the drugs hadn't kicked in yet, but everything felt more intense. Fantasies of Maggie in my dorm room flooded my head. Many times I'd thought about her doing this to me, but had chickened out on making a move.

A slow drag of her teeth returned me to the moment. Normally, I'd stop her and return the favor before moving on to other things, but today was different. Middle of the afternoon and the whole night stretched before us. A whole night with no plans. No agenda. And hopefully, no trip the ER in four and a half hours.

I gently rested my hand on her head, not directing or commanding, driven only by the need for more contact and connection. The tingling she joked about began low in my spine. I focused on dragging out my pleasure as I felt the point of no return getting closer. I closed my eyes and tried to think of droids and annoying animated sidekicks. I concentrated on picturing epic battles and the smiting of evil overlords. Instead, my brain conjured up strawberry blond hair and breasts barely contained by swirls of gold. I opened my eyes and realized she was staring at me. The passion I could see in her eyes, the love, pushed me over the edge. My fingers tightened around the strands of her hair as my hips arched forward, seeking more, as I exploded.

I let my head fall back on the bed. Her hands rested on my thighs for a brief moment before she flopped next to me.

"Hi," she whispered, her eyes sparkling with self-satisfaction.

"Hi." I touched her cheek and leaned down to kiss her.

"Feeling anything yet?"

"Oh, I'm feeling something. That was amazing."

She rolled to her side and wrapped a leg over mine. "I meant do you feel different?"

I paused to think about it, taking inventory of my body. I felt satisfied, but not satiated. "I don't feel done for the night, if that's what you're asking."

She grinned at me and I mirrored her expression.

My hand moved down her body, cupping her through her jeans. "You're wearing too many clothes."

"Let's fix that."

Once naked, I returned the favor. I teased her, nipping at the skin of her inner thighs and hipbones, making her squirm. I took my time, enjoying the feel of her arousal on my tongue. Slowly, I built up the pressure and rhythm until she came undone against my mouth.

I kissed the soft skin of her stomach and then licked my lips to taste where she lingered there.

Maggie lay against the pillows, languid and flushed. Seeing her blissed out, and knowing I did that to her, stirred my own desire again. A low hum began to build in my blood. It hadn't been that long, but I was ready for round two. Maggie noticed the evidence when it brushed against her thigh.

"Oh, hello." She reached out her hand and grasped me in greeting. "Nice to see you again."

"Are you shaking hands with my penis?"

"I am. Less rude than a leg poking." She gave me a sidelong look. "Up for another round?"

The hum turned into a buzz. "Definitely."

Her grip tightened and she stroked me a few times. I didn't need the encouragement. I felt rock hard and more than ready.

She rolled to her side and shifted so her leg rested on my hip, opening herself to me. Lessening her grip, she rubbed my tip against her slickness. I couldn't stand it, I had to be inside her. Gripping her hip, I thrust into her and rolled her on top of me.

She leaned forward to kiss me and I reached for her breasts, letting their weight fill my hands. When she sat back, my hands remained on her as I squeezed and brushed my thumbs over her nipples. She controlled the pace and angle in this position. I loved watching her chase her pleasure while she moved above me.

Her hair tumbled down her back when she arched her neck and her movement began to lose its rhythm. I knew she was getting close again and reached between us to press my thumb against her, giving her that extra stimulation she needed.

I felt her begin to clench and flutter inside. Her hand replaced mine on her breast, adding to her pleasure as she rocked with her orgasm.

I was still hard and inside her.

Maggie's orgasms today: two and counting.

CHAPTER 3

MAGGIE

Maybe it was the pills. Maybe it was all that talk of college Gil. Or the Star Wars pillowcase and sexy Princess Leia. Or maybe it was my eternal Hans Solo crush I failed to mention last night. Whatever the reason, we didn't get much sleep. I wasn't sure I could walk this morning.

When Gil stirred beside me and threw his arm over my waist, I tensed, thinking the pills hadn't worn off yet and he'd want to go for round … four? I tried to recall if that was the shower or the sofa. I'd lost track of my orgasms after the dining room table. I was attempting to count them when his hand cupped my breast.

"Morning," he whispered into my hair.

"Mmmorning," I mumbled. "I'm hoping you can walk this morning. I'm not sure I can get out of bed to make coffee. Or do any of the things."

He chuckled.

"Listen, Mr. Smug." I rolled over to face him.

"Yes, Ms. Satisfied?" He reached for my hip, wrapping his hand around the curve.

"Don't get any ideas."

"About?" His forehead wrinkled, but his focus remained on his hand, now caressing my skin.

"I'm serious about the not being able to walk."

He grinned at me. "Sorry."

"No, you're not."

"Not at all. Although, I have to admit, I'm not sure I could handle anything this morning."

I moved my hand toward the juncture of his legs.

He grabbed it before I could make contact with him. He kissed my palm. "Men get sore, too."

"Really?" I blinked at him.

"Yes, really. Can I confess something?"

"Sure."

"Last night was incredible."

"It was."

"I'm not finished." He tapped my nose. "But honestly? I'm not sure I ever want to repeat it."

Relief settled over me. "Thank God."

"You okay with just regular, boring, old sex with me?"

I could hear the undercurrent of insecurity beneath his question.

"I'm more than okay."

He exhaled and gently kissed me.

"Although, maybe every once and a while wouldn't be bad. Maybe a half dose?"

"If it makes you scream my name like you did in the living room, how could I say no? But maybe they should sell those pills along with packets of lube."

"Or gallon jugs."

"That would make picking up the prescription more than a little awkward."

Warmth spread across my cheeks imagining Gil standing in line at the drug store holding a gallon jug of lube. Maybe it would have a pump dispenser for convenience. "We could stick with oysters."

"Speaking of food, I'm starved," he said.

"Me, too." I stretched and groaned. "Donuts?"

"Stay in bed, I'll get them." He kissed me again and got up. His back cracked when he stretched, causing us both to laugh at our forty-something bodies recovering from a night of twenty-something sex. It would take days for us to recover from last night's escapades.

CHAPTER 4

MAGGIE

After a quick shower, I made my way downstairs to the kitchen for ibuprofen and water. Selah's gift bag still sat on the counter. We had forgotten to open her real gift. With mixed feelings about another sex related present, I slowly peeled off the black and white striped wrapping paper.

A silver-framed Polaroid sat nestled amongst black tissue inside the box. My breath hitched. Seven smiling faces, arms thrown over shoulders, the sun creating a golden shadow across the crowns of our heads, our youth had been captured and frozen forever. Or as long as Polaroids lasted.

Jo's blonde hair glowed in the bright light. Ben focused his eyes on her and not the camera. Selah and Quinn wore nearly identical plaid shirts over cut-off jeans and matching combat boots. In the middle stood Gil with his arm casually tossed over my shoulder, his hand resting on Lizzy's head. My head was tossed back and my eyes were squeezed closed with laughter. A look of pure amusement danced in Gil's eyes. He must have said something funny just as the picture was snapped.

Barely legible, "these are the days" was written in Selah's

distinct cursive on the border. The ink had faded over the subsequent decades into a pool of smudged blue.

I raised the frame closer to examine the picture. My finger traced over Lizzy's face through the glass. A soft sigh escaped as a small wave of loss lapped at my heart.

When I glanced up, Gil stood in the doorway watching me. "What did she give us?"

He set the bag of donuts on the counter. I could smell the still warm maple bacon bar.

I turned the frame to face him.

"Where did she ever find this?" He took the picture from my hands and smiled. "Geez, look at us. We look like the cast of *Singles*."

"Or the cast of *Singles* looked like us." I sipped from the large latte he'd brought me.

"Probably more apt."

"Your hair was so long." I pointed out where his hair hit his shoulders.

"Maybe I should grow it out again. Be that professor who wears a pony tail and has a beanbag in my office."

"Maybe not." I shook my head and frowned.

"You haven't changed." He lowered his voice.

"You're full of shit."

"Not the parts of you that count." He tapped the glass, his eyes filled with love. "That's the girl who stole my heart."

"She didn't know she had it." I leaned into his shoulder.

"Silly girl."

"That silly girl became the woman who gave me her heart."

"Smart woman." Our eyes locked and I knew what that girl in the picture hadn't. My heart would be safe with this man.

TAKE FOR GRANTED

A MODERN LOVE STORY SHORT

INTRODUCTION

Written as part of the "snow" themed LOL Anthology, I wanted to give Ben and Jo a sexy story to prove married couples can have still have fun together years after their HEA. When I wrote the sexy bartender Jo flirts with at the hotel bar, I had zero idea readers would fall for him and demand he get his own book. Who knew a sexy accent and a man bun would be so enticing!

Jo and Ben Grant are spending a week in Aspen.
Without their three kids.
It'll be bliss.
Heaven.
Finally, they'll have time alone to reconnect with each other. Jo wants spice things up to get them out of their marriage rut. When she plans a wild evening out, will Ben embrace the crazy?
Readers first met Ben and Jo in *We Were Here* and *Geoducks Are for Lovers*.
This short is the first appearance of Stan from *Next to You*.

PROLOGUE

Vail 2011: Ear infection and altitude sickness
Whistler 2012: Sinus infection
Park City 2013: Bronchitis
Darien 2014: Flu
Aspen 2015: Lingering cough since the holidays

I'm cursed.

Every year we plan a family ski trip over winter break in February, and every single year I get sick. Every, single damn year. Instead of schwooping down the slopes or going out to eat, I sleep in the condo and get familiar with on-call doctors, local Urgent Care facilities, and pharmacies.

Need a good pharmacy in Vail?

Doctor with long hours in Park City?

I'm your girl.

This year is going to be different.

All three kids are going to Florida with my parents.

That means it will only be Ben and I. In Aspen. Together. Alone.

No condo with multiple bedrooms and a kitchen. Every mom

on "vacation" knows there's some expectation of cooking something if there's a kitchen. Condos also come with laundry rooms. Cooking and doing laundry are not a vacation. Vacation means relaxation and escape. Not washing mounds of dirty underwear.

Did I mention I'm the mother of three teenagers?

No kids means we'll be in a hotel room, a suite, with housekeeping, and room service, and turn down service, and nothing for me to do.

In other words, heaven.

Ben has a couple meetings scheduled during the trip. Meetings that will take place on the mountain or in the gondola while they pretend to ski. Other than the meetings and a client dinner, we have no plans. No schedule.

No kids. No schedule. No chores.

A week of bliss.

I am not going to get sick.

I've been chugging chalky Vitamin C powder and swallowing extra vitamins and zinc for the past two months to ward off germs and evil viruses.

Flu shot, Vitamin B12 shot, wheatgrass shots… I'd done all that I could in preparation for this trip.

I will not get sick.

I will not get sick.

My view out the window tips from sky to earth. My stomach lurches when the plane banks a sharp turn over the rocky, snow dusted peaks of the Rockies on the short flight from Denver to Aspen.

"Doesn't this make you think of that movie *Alive*?" I ask Ben.

He's reading the Wall Street Journal like he's sitting at his desk at work, completely undisturbed by the fact that we are careening over jagged mountains at a high speed.

"The nineties one about the soccer players who crashed in the Andes?" he asks into his paper.

"Yes, that's the one." I gently clench his wrist as the plane bounces on an updraft.

"You're morbid. Wasn't Ethan Hawke in that? Did he survive?" His eyes flick to my face.

"I'm not morbid. If you put down the paper for a second and looked outside, you'd agree." I push down the paper with my other hand. "And of course Ethan survived. I couldn't watch his movies for years without thinking 'cannibal' in my head every time I saw him."

"Right, I remember that. You had a hard time deciphering

reality from fiction and acting back then." He ducks his head and leans across my seat to see the view. "Yep, exactly like the Andes."

"Life rule number one: don't fly over the Andes in a small plane in the winter. Do you think the Rockies should be added to that?"

"Really?" He leans back and shakes out his paper before folding it in half and then half again. "That's still life rule number one? Not save the children and animals in a house fire? Or honor you marriage vows?" His wedding ring catches the sunlight through the window as he holds up his hand.

"Those are givens, no rule needed." I lift his wrist and kiss the platinum band.

"We could always make the three hour drive back to Denver next weekend. Avoid any chance of me turning into Ethan Hawke." He kisses my cheek.

I frown and turn to kiss his lips. "You've aged much better."

His laugh makes his small paunch jiggle. It's not really fair to call it a paunch, but it wasn't there in his thirties, and definitely not in his twenties. Other than a few gray hairs at his temples and a slightly higher forehead, he's still a damn handsome man. Maybe even the "d" word: distinguished.

"Good to know." He returns to his paper.

The flight attendant walks through the small cabin, reminding us to return our seats to their upright position and stow our blah, blah blah. I notice her hand pauses on Ben's seatback a little longer than the others. Her "Mr. Grant" comes out like a purr.

Hello, I'm sitting right next to him and he's wearing a ring.

I should be used to this. Younger women see men like my husband as catches. Established, wealthy, successful men like Ben have an aura of confidence women find appealing. Wives and family be damned.

Good luck, sister. I snort.

Ben casts me a sidelong look and hands his paper to the lingering stewardess. I roll my eyes and return to my window.

After few more bounces, sways and turns, the plane finds the narrow strip of flat ground that is the Aspen airport. I think about kissing the tarmac when we walk down the stairs until the cold late afternoon wind hits me. "Brr, it's cold" I shiver and wrap my down parka tightly around myself.

"Sure you wouldn't rather be in Florida where it's warm?" Ben shouts over the noise from the jet and the wind.

"And miss out on the hot toddies, hot tubs and hot men? No way!"

He laughs, knowing there's no way I'd ever get in a public hot tub. Not even at a five star hotel.

Our driver looks like he moved here in the seventies and never left. Part hippie, part skier, he's wearing an old school ski sweater with deep blue snowflakes on a cream background. The car has a faint scent of cannabis beneath the cheery pine scent from the tree air-freshener hanging from the rearview mirror

Ben meets my eyes and gestures like he's smoking. "Doobie," he whispers as if the pantomime and scent weren't enough for me to figure out the connection.

"You like the Doobie brothers?" Darren, the driver, smiles at us in the rearview mirror. "Me too."

I have to look out the window to avoid bursting into giggles.

Luckily it's a short drive to The Little Nell Hotel, our home for the week. Located at the base of Ajax and the gondolas, The Nell is an Aspen institution. Our suite has a four-poster bed and a separate living area, both with incredible views of the mountain, currently tinged indigo with the setting sun. A fire glows in the fireplace, giving the effortlessly chic room a cozy feeling.

I eye the bed and all sorts of salacious thoughts run through my head about putting the posts to good use. I've read too many books. Ben's no dominant. Other than the occasional spank or slap, he'd probably think I'm crazy if I suggested anything kinky.

Sighing, I walk into the enormous bathroom and set my cosmetics bag on the counter. The light is flattering, giving a glow to my blond highlights and hiding my faint crows' feet. I wiggle my eyebrows. The Botox is beginning to wear off, but my forehead is still smooth.

I don't look forty-something. Mid-thirties tops. I resist the urge to examine my face closer, knowing I'll still be closer to fifty than thirty no matter how youthful my skin looks.

The sound of Bloomberg TV carries in from the bedroom. I lean back to see Ben flopped on the bed, remote in his hand, business chatter flowing from the flat screen. We could be at home.

"We have a dinner reservation at eight. I'm going to take a shower," I call over to him.

"Great." He picks up his phone and texts something.

Great. I sweep my shoulder length hair into a bun and turn on the enormous shower.

"Plenty of room for two in the shower," I shout.

When there's no response, I peek out of the bathroom. Ben's on his phone and holds up his finger for silence.

You can take the man away from the office, but these days, you can't take the office away from the man.

It's Friday evening and I'm going to make the most of it. Maybe I'll be able to lure him out dancing later. If not tonight, I have a plan for tomorrow night that should end with us screwing each other's brains out like we used to do in college.

Dried, moisturized, and made-up, I pull my hair out of its bun, letting the blond waves fall around my shoulders in a perfect tousled mess for dinner tonight.

From the faint sound of his voice, Ben's moved his call to the living room, and closed the door to the bedroom.

I unpack and hang our clothes in the closet, and put things in the drawers. Tonight's outfit is a slim pair of dark jeans and a black cashmere tunic. It's lightly snowing out and I debate heels or boots. Heels win because I doubt we'll leave the hotel.

Ben finally ends his call and declares he's going to take a shower. His hand trails over my shoulder and down to the slight curve of my hip as he passes. The gesture is habitual, but sends a current through my body.

"You look beautiful," he whispers despite it being the two of us.

I smile and thank him, but he's already in the bathroom.

I sit on the bed and flip through channels, but nothing catches my attention. I'm in Aspen. There must be more interesting things to do than watch reruns on Bravo.

Over the noise of the shower, I shout, "I'm going downstairs. I'll meet you in the bar."

He says he'll meet me there. At least I think that's what he says as the steam shower begins to fog.

ownstairs the aprés ski crowd is buzzing, swarming the cozy living room style lounge where a fire roars in the large stone fireplace. I find a seat at the end of the long bar in the restaurant. Like our suite, it's beyond chic with traditional and modern styles mixed together. Deep blues and light grays highlight the narrow space. The lighting is soft and everyone looks like they walked out of a fashion magazine. Faux and real fur accent both women and men, diamonds glitter, and casual looking ski clothes probably cost a fortune.

While waiting for the bartender's attention, I spin my three-carat engagement ring, an upgrade from the classic one-carat Ben proposed with after business school.

Of course, the bartender is beautiful, too. He's either a snowboarder or model. Probably both. He has a neatly trimmed beard and, according to Ella, a man bun. Leave it to the thirteen year old to know more about fashion and trends than her mom.

Man bun or not, he's gorgeous with his dark hair and pale skin. And I am staring. To occupy myself while I wait, I chomp on a handful of buttery Spanish marcona almonds from the small dish on the bar.

I study the cocktail list until a deep baritone asks, "Can I get you something?"

My eyes meet with clear blue. He has to be a model. "Um…" I pause, every name for every alcoholic concoction leaving my head. "I'll have…" I stare at the fuzzy words in front of me.

"What do you like? I'll make you something special. Vodka? Bourbon? Tequila? Gin?"

I frown at gin. Gin and I broke up many years ago, and we will never ever, ever get back together.

"Vodka." I meet his intense eyes and smile.

"Are you a sweet or salty girl?" He leans on his forearm in front of me.

I know he's asking about my drink preferences, but his flirting with patrons skill is impressive.

"Sweet." It comes out as a husky, secret-sharing whisper.

"Citrus?"

"Yes."

"Do you like a little spice?"

I nod. The muscles of his forearms where he's rolled up the cuffs of his shirt distract me from actual speech.

I note his fingers, neatly trimmed nails, and an expensive vintage watch. He only has a smattering of hair on his arms. I wonder if he has chest hair. I mentally slap myself for imagining his naked chest. Or cataloguing the barest glimpse of his skin like it's my job.

Married, not blind. No harm in looking.

"I have the perfect thing." He pushes back from the counter and I have the urge to fan myself.

His nimble hands and fingers grab bottles, squeeze lemon and muddle sugar. I think he adds ginger and maybe a bit of red pepper to the shaker. My focus moves up to his biceps as he shakes the silver container with vigor.

So much enthusiasm and energy goes into the mixing of my cocktail. It reminds me of a jackrabbit.

I wonder if he'd be fast like that in bed.

Young, full of energy, and too good looking to ever be told he was awful in bed could be a terrible combination.

He gently twists a thin slice of lemon peel before carefully setting it on the edge of the chilled martini glass he's placed in front of me. He pours the honey colored liquid slowly into the frosty glass, filling it almost to the edge, but not spilling a single drop.

It's the single most erotic thing I've witnessed in ages.

I clearly don't get out enough.

He clears his throat and I realize he's waiting for me to taste his concoction. I worry my hands might shake too much to lift the glass, so I lean forward, and take a small sip.

I close my eyes as the sweet, intense flavor hits my tongue followed by the zing of heat despite the icy temperature of the drink.

"It's amazing." I lick the corner of my lips before slowly opening my eyes.

"Thank you. I love watching someone enjoy something I make."

I slowly blink at him. It must be the lack of oxygen, but one sip of alcohol has me feeling light and giddy.

"Can I open a tab for you? Or charge it to your room?" His voice has a slight accent I can't place. Could be South African or Australian. Or New Zealand.

I give him our suite number and tell him to leave it open. He moves down the bar to help other customers, including a loud, giggling group of snow bunnies. They lean over the bar to flirt with him, exposing the cleavage barely hidden by their low-cut sweaters.

He laughs and acts the part with them, but his glance keeps finding mine. He gives me a knowing smile and rolls his eyes when he reaches behind the bar to pour them another glass of prosecco.

I could probably be the girls' mother.

It's a sobering thought, and I finish my cocktail in a long swallow. I twist the stem of the martini glass, chastising myself for flirting with a bartender.

Or wanting to.

I love my husband.

And here comes the but… but after twenty-years of the same man and the same penis and the same sex, we're in a rut.

We've probably been in this rut for years, but I've been in the haze of kids for a decade. With teenagers comes the realization that soon, we'll be a pair again, and that's a little strange.

"Can I get you another? Or something different?" Gorgeous and off limits asks.

"Another." I smile with my lips closed.

He sets up to make my drink in front of me, rather than work near the gaggle of twenty-somethings. "Where are you from?"

"Connecticut. At least now."

He raises an eyebrow.

"We've moved around."

"Me too," he says, flashing a row of perfectly white teeth. They remind me of a shark. I bet he has a long list of one-night stands around the world.

"I was trying to place your accent." I admit, then feel my cheeks heat.

"Cape Town."

Not a Kiwi. For some reason, this disappoints me.

"What brought you to Aspen?" I can't help my curiosity. The attention and ability to stare at his gorgeous face feeds my interest.

"Rugby."

That's a surprise. "Not the mountains?"

He gives me a shy smile. "Rugby's my first love, but I do all right on the slopes."

And off, I think. Rugby player? Could he get any hotter? I feel flushed, and I'm not sure if it's the flirting, the alcohol, or an impending hot flash.

"And you?"

I blink at him, having no idea what he's asking.

"Me what?"

"What brings you to Aspen?"

"The typical… vacation, skiing." Husband, but I don't say that part out loud. I'm wearing my wedding set, so it's not like I'm trying to hide that I'm married. Although my left hand is hidden on my lap. It's rude to put elbows on tables and bars.

"First time?"

Flirting with a hot bartender? No.

"No, we've been here before. For years, we stayed in Snowmass, so it's nice to be in Aspen again." Snowmass is code for family vacation with its abundance of condos and easier trails for beginners. I wonder if he'll pick up on it.

He shakes my cocktail and I stare at his arms again. I notice a shadow of black peeking out from under his left cuff. It looks thick and tribal. My mind imagines dark bands wrapping around muscle and curling up his arm to his shoulder.

"Do you still play?" I attempt to make conversation.

"Rugby? Yeah. But I'm getting old." He sets my fresh drink in front of me.

I snort and cover my mouth with my hand.

He laughs, deep and masculine. The sound washes over me and I cross my legs impulsively.

"It's true. It's a difficult sport on the body."

Images of tough, thick male bodies covered in mud, thrashing and tackling each other on a field come to mind. I purse my lips and exhale, slow and steady, trying to calm my heart rate.

It must be the altitude and lack of oxygen, but this nameless bartender has my head spinning. Not that I would ever do anything with him, but in a few short sentences, he's done more for my libido than porn or erotica have for months.

Where's Ben? Remembering I do have a husband and he should be down here by now, I scan the long bar area for his familiar brown hair. The crowd is beginning to thin as people move on to dinner reservations or naps before a night of clubbing. I'd love to go dancing again. It's been ages.

"Where's the best place to dance in town this year?" I ask Mr. Rugby, who is lingering near me.

"What kind of dancing? Crazy club stuff with foam? Or honky-tonk with a live band?" He gives me a list of both types, listing some old Aspen standbys and new places.

I snicker at honky-tonk and then cover it up with sipping my cocktail.

"Don't you say honky-tonk?" he smiles and leans back.

"Not in Connecticut. Texas maybe. I've never been to one."

"No? Line dancing and country songs?" He studies my face. "No, you don't seem the type."

"Oh, really? Go on." I sip and wait for his assessment.

He puts his elbow on the bar in front of me and tips his head. "The type who doesn't go to honky-tonk bars. Or clubs. Or sits alone at bars."

He's close enough that I can smell his cologne and his man scent. He gives good pheromones.

"Am I close?"

Too close. I shift away from him. "You're very observant."

"It's part of my job. Plus, I studied psychology at university. Comes into good use for playing rugby, and bartending."

A jock and smart. I set down my glass and settle into my seat. "Well, you've figured me out."

"You're more difficult to read than most women who sit here alone."

"What does that mean?"

He picks up a bar cloth and wipes down the counter to my right where two seats have opened. He places fresh bowls of almonds out for the next patrons.

"You seem fine being alone. Happy about it even. Most single women have a slight edge of …" His words fade out as he thinks of the adjective he wants.

"Desperation? Sadness? Loneliness?" I fill in the blank he's left.

He smirks and moves a bowl of almonds in front of me. "Maybe all three? Some women are all about the hunt, the game, the flirtation."

Put me in the last category. I've enjoyed chatting with him and his attention a little too much.

"Some act like they'll never get asked to dance, so they curl up and feel sorry for themselves. Won't even make eye-contact."

I find myself locking eyes with him. He smirks.

"It must be fascinating."

He gets called down to the gaggle of girls. They giggle and touch his arms where they rest on the bar. They're bold and far more direct than I've ever been with men. Although it's been decades since I was on the hunt.

A man slips into the seat next to me. His body heat fills the space. I glance over out of curiosity, and am met with familiar brown eyes.

"Hi," I whisper, my cheeks warming.

"Hello, Mrs. Grant." His arm rests on the low back of my stool. "You're beautiful when you smile and flirt."

Caught, I give him a deer in the headlights look.

"No need to be guilty. I've enjoyed watching you."

"You have?" I swallow. "From where?"

He points to a small table with a banquette in the corner behind me. I didn't see him when I scanned the bar earlier.

"How long have you been here?" I ask.

"Long enough." His fingers play down my spine and splay across the base, right above my ass. "You're the most beautiful woman in here." His breath skims across my skin right before he kisses my cheek near my ear.

My gaze flicks to his and then down the bar.

"He's very handsome, but what's with the bun?" Ben asks, munching on some almonds.

"Ella calls them man buns."

"Looks like something Gil would have worn in college in that grunge band."

I chuckle, but nod. "He so would've."

The rugby god returns to us and, without missing a beat or looking surprised that I'm no longer alone, asks for Ben's drink order. A Manhattan up. Always.

I catch myself watching Rugby's arms again. I can't help it.

Another perfect cocktail is poured in front of us.

"Thanks…" Ben pauses, waiting for a name.

"Stan."

"Thank you, Stan. Excellent drink."

Stan. Stanley.

Not a sexy name. At all.

My fantasy begins to fade with reality. Fantasies are best kept to the imagination.

We drink our cocktails and Ben chatters about his conference call and business dinner. The familiarity of his voice lulls me, soothing the heat building under my skin.

"Shall we?" he asks.

"What?"

"Dinner?"

"Yes."

Ben settles up our tab, thanking Stan for keeping me company. I give a little wave when we walk past him and the gang of available women. I wonder which one will end up in his bed tonight.

Part of me says a silent thank you. I can't imagine having first time sex with someone new. All the awkwardness of not knowing what to expect, or discovering the weird foibles and fetishes of the other person.

I lean up and kiss Ben's cheek as we walk through the restaurant to our table.

"What was that for?"

"For being my forever."

"You're not leaving me and the kids for Stan the Man… bun?" He gives me his serious face.

"It never crossed my mind." I reassure him, knowing it isn't necessary.

As we sit and eat, I hatch a plan for the weekend. I realize my relationship ennui isn't about wanting something else; it's about wanting something fresh.

And I have the perfect plot to give us a little spark.

*B*en puts on his ridiculously brightly colored red parka, gloves and ski pants while I laugh at him from the sofa.

"It's in case I go off trail and into the woods. I want them to find my unconscious body as quickly as possible."

"Stop!" I can't breathe from laughing at him so hard. "That's a terrible thing to think about."

"If I told you the guy at the ski shop sold me this outfit this morning because I told him to give me what all the cool snowboarders are wearing these days, you might asphyxiate yourself with laughter."

I stop laughing and hold my hand over my mouth. "No."

He nods and spins for me. "I'm worried I'll run into some X Games champion in the same jacket. Who would that be more embarrassing for?"

I fall off the sofa in a fit of cackling snorts. "What was wrong with your North Face stuff? Isn't that still cool?"

"It's too east coast or last year, or something." He checks out the wild pattern of his jacket in the mirror. "I look like a moron."

"But you'll be the first one found. I'll be able to spot you from our window. Or the après ski deck."

He laughs at himself and pulls out his coordinating gloves. He's the most ridiculous vision of a middle age man trying too hard.

"Hold on!" I run into the bedroom to grab my phone. "Pose," I tell him as my finger hovers, ready to take his pic.

"No social media." He makes a serious face and at the last minute adds duck lips.

The picture is blurry from my laughter. "Stop. Just be serious."

I snap another pic and text it to the kids. "I promise, no social media, but I might have to send it to Maggie and Selah." My best friends from college will get a laugh over the guy they dubbed Mr. Republican in freshman year.

"Fine." He kisses my cheek, but I turn and catch his lips for a real kiss. His surprise makes him pause, before returning it and swiping his tongue into my mouth. We kiss and he wraps his arm around my back.

This is no peck hello or good-bye. This is a real, sexual, could start something that might lead somewhere kiss. He ends it too soon.

"Wow. Where'd that come from?" His breath is shallow.

"I'm not sure. It might be the outfit." My lips twitch as I fight my laughter. "But there is more of that for later. I have big plans for us tonight."

"You do? What are these plans?" He taps my nose with his index finger.

"Not telling. But I'll be confiscating your phone at seven sharp. No business on a Saturday night."

"Yes, ma'am." He kisses me again, a familiar peck, but that's okay.

I keep my mouth closed and kiss him back with a little more pressure. "You better leave before I strip you out of this clown suit and have my way with you."

"Can I still wear the hat?" He backs away to the door, pulling his ridiculous pom-pom adorned hat over his eyes.

"Be safe out there this morning. I'll meet you at one for lunch." I turn and walk into the bedroom.

While he skis and talks business, I'll be having a massage and shopping. I have some things to pick up for tonight and there's the perfect little lingerie shop a few blocks away.

Massage over, I feel loose and noodley. The glass of prosecco after probably enhances whatever endorphins or dopamine my brain is releasing.

Again, I think the lack of oxygen up here has something to do with it. Bright sunshine, not enough oxygen, and I'm feeling good.

Really good. So good that when my mother texts from Florida with an update I don't even have the urge to call and micro-manage their day.

Definitely must be high from the altitude.

I glide down the street, window-shopping all the incredible designer shops. Knowing Ben, his skiing ensemble probably cost more than new skis in this town.

Arriving at the small alley, I duck down to the white door that encloses the most beautiful lingerie shop. Discreet, European and outrageously expensive, it's everything I love.

The saleswoman helps me pick out a few pieces and measures me to make sure I get the right size. She offers me another glass of prosecco, and I accept. As she wraps my purchase in the silver tissue, a case of toys catches my eye. I tell her to wait and walk over to the display.

She explains the line of products without embarrassment or judgment. I buy three things, which she also wraps in tissue before placing them in a plain white bag, the shop's equivalent of brown paper. It's completely bland, but if you know this shop, immediately recognizable.

I receive a small smile and nod from the doorman when he greets me back at the hotel. I'm certain I catch his eye on the bag. I mumble a thank you and enter the elevator. The woman in the car with me nods and smiles. "I love their things."

So much for discreet. I give her a smile in return. We've formed an immediate bond.

In the room, I unwrap everything and tuck it away for later tonight.

I join Ben and his business associates for lunch. There's a lot of shop talk. All four men wear brightly colored ski ensembles. I wonder if they all had the same sales associate, and if he works on commission.

I tune out their talk and face the sun, letting the strong rays heat my cheeks. Through the dark lenses of my sunglasses, I watch snowboarders and skiers fly down the mountain towards us. The patio is crowded with people taking a break from the slopes. Chatter about conditions and expected overnight snow mix with dreams of deep powder in the morning. It's a foreign language to my ears. I begin to drift off.

"Jo?" Ben's voice sounds far away. "Honey?"

I realize I'm half asleep at the table. I rouse myself and sit up, removing my sunglasses. "I apologize. I think the altitude is affecting me." And two proseccos before lunch, but I don't say that part out loud.

Ben and the men don't seem offended when they announce they're heading back up the mountain for a few more runs. One of them, I think his name is Neal, tells us about a pop-up champagne bar.

My ears perk up. "That sounds like my kind of skiing," I say. "Maybe tomorrow. This afternoon, I need a nap."

The group chuckles as I excuse myself. All of them stand when I leave the table. For some strange reason, I give a slight bow.

Ben raises his eyebrows at me and presses his lips together to keep from smiling. Or laughing. I bow to him again before saying goodbye to push his buttons. His jaw ticks with the effort he is using not to laugh.

I roll myself up in one of the hotel robes before crawling into the down-covered bed. I feel like a marshmallow inside a giant jar of Fluff.

I'm weightless, ageless, and carefree as I drift into sleep.

It's dark outside when I open my eyes. I hear the TV from the other room and Ben's lowered voice. It's Saturday, but the man never stops working.

I vow to put his phone in the room's safe for tonight. I stretch in my Fluff cave. My inner sloth debates whether we should get room service and stay in after all.

One Saturday night.

One.

I get one Saturday night on this trip in Aspen.

My inner twenty-something shouts at me. She's very bossy, so I listen to her and crawl out of the warmth of Fluffland. I pad over to the door and listen to Ben drone on about reports and projections.

I'll take a shower, no a bath, and hope he's off by the time I'm done. I check the clock and see it's five. Plenty of time to soak for a bit.

I'm surrounded by bubbles in the jetted tub when Ben walks in with a glass of wine for me.

"Hi, sleeping beauty." He hands me the glass and kisses my head. "Good nap?"

"Hi, handsome." His outrageous ski clothes have been replaced with lounge pants and a thin sweater. So much better.

He sits at the end of the tub. "What's the plan for tonight?"

I swallow a cool sip of pinot noir. "Nice try. Dinner at the Jerome and then I'm not telling. Wear jeans. No clown suits."

"Should I wear a shirt?"

I splash some bubbles on his leg.

He jumps away. "Fine, shirt and jeans. I'll be ready."

When I finish in the bathroom, Ben is sitting on the sofa in dark jeans and a charcoal gray shirt with the cuffs rolled up.

I'm in leggings with leather tuxedo stripes and a flowy, coral pink blouse that stops at my hips. Underneath is a lace bodysuit with boning and built-in bra. From the outside it's invisible, but I hope Ben discovers it while we're out. Short boots and my black faux fur vest finish off the outfit. Ben pauses when he sees me.

"You're the most beautiful woman in any room."

I smile. "I'm the only woman in the room, but thank you."

"I said any room. And I meant it." He stands. I walk to him, wrapping my arms around him. In my boots, we're closer in height.

"I love you," I whisper into his neck.

"I love you, too." His arms meet at the base of my back and he squeezes me. "Let's go."

I grab my floppy black hat and a scarf as big as a blanket to wrap around my neck for the short distance to Hotel Jerome.

As we walk through the charming streets of Aspen, a light

snow begins to fall, dusting us both in large flakes. Ben stops in the glowing lights from a shop to kiss me.

"What was that for?"

"I don't know." He shakes his head. "It must be the snow, but something about tonight makes me feel twenty-years younger. I want to kiss you in the street, push you up against the side of a building, and make anyone who sees us jealous."

His words cause my breath to hitch. He hasn't spoken like that in years. It didn't matter in college if we were alone or in a room full of people. We'd kiss and try to crawl under each other's skin if we could, never able to get close enough.

As tempting as making out in the snow against a building sounds, I'm beginning to freeze, so I tug him behind me down the sidewalk.

CHAPTER 4

"Where are we going?" he asks as I steer us down yet another street lined with brick buildings after dinner. It's a little before ten and we're tipsy from cocktails and wine. Laughing, I stumble on my heels, but he catches me before I can tilt toward the ground.

I intertwine our fingers as we traverse the cobblestones along Hyman Avenue toward our destination. When Stan told me the name last night, I knew it was too good to pass up. Escobar, named for the infamous Colombian coke kingpin, was not only the hottest dance club in town, but also a tongue-in-cheek nod to Aspen's own long history with South American snow.

Ben seems delighted by the name, but a little wary of the ultra-hip club. He pauses outside as yet another gaggle (school? pride? murder?) of snow bunnies giggle their way past us.

I pull his hand. "Come dance with me. It'll be fun. I promise."

He relents and pays the cover.

We're the oldest people by a decade, at least, but I don't care. We find a tiny table and order expensive cocktails that aren't half as good as Stan's. Electronic dance music pulses in the small space. The small dance area is half-filled. Bodies grind with the pulsating beat.

Ben extends his hand and we join the fray. It's tight and we're old, but I don't care. I dance like I'm twenty and kidless. I dance like I'm seducing my date for the first time.

We move like a couple who knows each other, but tonight our energy is different. I can feel an undercurrent of anticipation. I'm going to get laid tonight. Hotel sex laid.

Ben's energy has changed too. He's dominant and territorial, touching me, moving against me in a way he never does anymore.

Wearing the bodysuit all night has not been my best decision. It's the kind of seductive lingerie that should be worn for the briefest period of time before being torn from the body.

The lace is beginning to chafe a little. The boning pokes a rib. A big part of my dancing is finding a way to alleviate the awkward feeling of having a row of snaps across my vagina.

Finally, Ben's hands sweep over my hips and under my shirt. They pause for a beat.

This is the moment. Will my self-torture be worth it?

I sway my hips and place my hands over his, encouraging him.

He moves higher, feeling the lace between our skin. His fingers sweep over the curves of my breasts and his thumbs circle my nipples. We're pressed together so tightly, no one can see what he is doing despite being surrounded by people. The idea turns me on and I moan, tipping my head back and letting my hair sway behind me.

His lips brush my ear and he says, "What's this mischief?" as he pinches my nipples through the thin lace.

I turn to speak into his ear. "Part of the evening's surprises." I nip the corner of his jaw before I lean back to see his eyes.

They are half-closed and intense with desire. He roughly clasps my hand and draws it between our bodies to let me feel his hardness through his jeans.

"Oh." I exhale. I squeeze him and his eyes fully close.

He narrows the small distance between us, trapping my hand. I stroke him as his palms wander beneath my blouse, down over my ass, which he cups, grinding himself and the snaps further into me. The sensation goes from unpleasant to oddly stimulating.

The blessing of being forty-something is that no one pays attention to us.

Ben and I are practically humping in the middle of this dance floor, and we're invisible. More bodies crowd in around us, creating a wall between us and anyone seated at the bar and tables. I wonder if I were wearing a skirt, if we could have sex right here and no one would notice.

As if reading my mind, Ben whispers into my ear. "We need to leave before I try to take you on a dance floor."

I need no further encouragement before I'm pushing through the crowd of hipsters and snow bunnies faster than a bargain hunter on Black Friday. We get our things from coat check and tumble out onto the street.

This time he does press me into the cold brick of a building around the corner. It's not private or dark, but we don't care.

Our kiss is messy and passionate, sloppy, and I couldn't care who sees us. However, I have more planned for tonight than making out like horny teenagers in the snow.

"Take me home," I say between kisses.

"That's too far. How about the hotel?" He breathes warm air over my neck.

"Deal."

We behave ourselves through the lobby and into the elevator, or so it would appear. Ben has his hand under my vest and traces lace patterns on my back.

When our door closes behind us, he says one word that ignites me.

"Strip."

I blink as he prowls toward me, backing me into the bedroom. "Now."

I shrug off my vest and pull my blouse over my head, exposing the black lace of the body suit and the boning of the bra. I kick off my boots before bending to slowly peel off the leggings. When all clothing is gone, I climb across the bed to where I've hidden the last surprises.

Behind me I can hear him removing his own boots and clothes. He's standing in his black boxer briefs when I turn around. His eyes widen when I lay out my purchases.

"Where did you get those?"

"A shop."

He blinks and reaches out a hesitant finger to stroke the suede of the small flogger. It's petite, pink and looks harmless, but I know from the quick lashes the saleswoman did on my arm, it packs a sting. Next to it sits a mask and a pair of small clamps that promise to blow my mind. I have to admit, they kind of terrify me.

"And the roach clips?" His eyes meet mine and I see excitement, but also confusion.

"Not roach clips. They're, um, for, um, mynipples," I mumble the last two words together into one.

"Really? Because I have pot."

"What? You do?"

"Yeah, the guy at the ski shop told me where to buy it. It's legal here."

"Wait, you have pot?"

"You have deviant sex toys. The pot is seeming like the lesser of the two."

"How much pot? And since when do you smoke pot again?"

"Just a joint. And I haven't smoked in ages. But it's legal here."

I flop on the bed. "You said that. So you want to get stoned?"

"You want me to pinch your nipples and hit you with that thing?"

I nod. "We can do both."

"Which one first?"

I eye the nipple clamps. "The pot."

He hops off the bed and walks into the closet.

"Can we smoke it in our room? I don't want to get kicked out of The Nell for drugs."

"We'll open the door to the balcony." He nods toward the living room.

I stare at him. We're doing this. Like college kids.

"Okay. But I'll freeze." I grab my fluffy robe and put it on. Ben dons one too and we turn into a snow-people couple.

"Matches?" I ask.

"Right." He goes back to the closet and gets a lighter. We sit cross-legged in the open door to the small balcony, wrapped in robes. Not weird or obvious at all.

He lights the joint and inhales, then coughs like he has coal miner's lung. It's not sexy, but it is funny.

I laugh until he passes it to me and I do the same. "Damn." I take a shallow breath to stop the coughing. "This burns."

He snickers and gestures for me to pass it back. He exhales a small cloud that billows over the railing and dissipates into the falling snow.

After two hits, the floaty feeling I remember returns. I haven't been really stoned since college. I giggle at nothing and he joins me.

"What's funny?" he asks.

"I have no idea." I laugh louder, tipping back into the room and lying on the carpet.

"Do you want more?" He holds the glowing joint near me.

"Just one more or I'll be too high for sex." I inhale, and keep from choking this time.

I sit up to blow the smoke outside then hand the joint back to him. I flop back on the carpet, but roll to the side away from the cold air.

I attempt to stand up by moving to all fours and feel the snaps of my bodysuit give way. It rolls up my torso like a window shade.

It's both horrifying and liberating at the same time.

Laughing, I lose my balance and end up on my belly on the floor.

"You okay?"

I turn my head to see he's standing over me. He's closed the door to the balcony and put out the joint.

I roll over and hold up my hand to get him to help me stand.

"I popped my snaps." I open my robe to show him, essentially flashing the mountain if anyone happened to be out there in the darkness.

"What's going on down there?" he leans toward me.

If it weren't for the tie of the robe keeping the bodysuit at my waist, it would be under my boobs by now. As it is, I'm pantsless in all senses and flashing my husband. I close the robe.

"Nothing to see here. Let's move along." I turn around and try to resnap myself, but it's super awkward due to the fact that I might be on my way to being incredibly stoned.

"What was that we smoked?" I ask, my words sticking in my mouth like honey.

"Marijuana," he says with a straight face, flopping on the sofa and pulling me down on top of him.

"I know, but was it military-industrial complex strength? Like from Nam or something?"

"What are you even saying?"

"I have no idea. I'm thinking that in about fifteen minutes it's a good thing we have a bar full of complimentary snacks and beverages."

"That is a very good thing."

I lean my head on his shoulder.

"Do you still want to have sex?"

Sex! I'd forgotten.

"Yes!" I jump up and run to the bedroom.

I strip off the fluffy soft goodness (so fluffy) and the snapping lace torture costume. I struggle with getting it over my head and tip on to the bed face first. Before I can right myself, he stands behind me, his thighs brush mine.

"Stay still."

I don't really have a choice. I'm bent at the waist, face down in a fluffy Fluff bed with my arms and shoulders bound by lace.

I wait for him to do something. And wait.

Finally, I turn my head to see him standing there staring at my ass, the flogger in his hand.

"Hello?"

"I don't think I can do this. I keep thinking of Monty Python and the Spanish Inquisition."

"That's not sexy." I frown, trying to scoot up the bed and lose the lace.

"You're the one who bought the torture devices."

"They're adult toys. We're adults. These are age appropriate." I pick up the nipple clamps that do indeed look like roach clips, but why would anyone need connected roach clips?

"You're not thinking of using those on me, are you?" He covers his tiny man-nipples with his hands.

I open and close the clamps like miniature alligator jaws. "I want to bite your nipples," I say in a creepy Boris Karloff voice.

"Why do you sound like Karl Rove?"

"I'm doing Boris Karloff."

"No, but you're doing a spot on Rove." He chuckles.

"Is it turning you on?" I lunge at his chest with a clamp.

He shrieks like a little girl and dodges the petite maws of pain. "Not sexy," he says from the other side of the room.

This is not going how I planned. At all.

I stand up, stark naked and walk over to where he's sitting in the chair. "I'm sorry for the Spanish Inquisition and the Rove. Let me make it up to you." I kneel in front of him, face level with his cotton covered penis. I stroke him, bringing him to life. I reach my hands under the waistband and tug away the fabric. He lifts his hips to allow me to remove his boxers.

I cup his balls with one hand and roll them around like a gambler with a giant pair of dice.

"What are you doing?"

"Shhh… I'm playing with your balls. They're so fun. How do men not play with them all day long." I make myself laugh. "Oh, wait, you do."

His hand stills mine. "You said something about a blow job?"

I don't remember saying anything, but I am on my knees making eye contact with his one-eyed-wonder. "Right, that." I wrap my hand around his semi-hard length and stroke.

His eyes watch me. "Use your mouth."

I stare back at him. Oh, right. "Right. I'm getting there. Shaking hands first."

I lower my mouth to the tip and kiss it. He moans.

I lick it like an ice cream from base to tip and he groans, but in a good way. I lick again and swirl my tongue around the top. This is fun. I smile and exhale a little puff of air over the tip before wrapping my lips around him and slowly descending toward the base. I suck and lick, kiss, use my teeth a little, and even blow, putting the blow in blow job.

I crack myself up and try to laugh with a mouthful of Ben, and nearly gag. I go back to the ice cream licks for a while.

"It's not a popsicle," he whispers.

"There's a reason it's called a job, you know." I swallow his length as much as I can stand, using my hand to cover the rest.

"Mmm… that's nice," he says from above.

I meet his eyes again and attempt a wink, which makes him laugh and bob in my mouth.

I sit back on my heels. "I don't think either of us is supposed to be laughing while I'm doing this."

"Or talking. Usually there's a lot less talking." He lifts my hands and pulls me up to standing.

"I'm really thirsty now." I walk, still naked, to the bar. I open a bag of tortilla chips, a tube of gummy bears, and a jar of almonds, and begin eating all three.

"I thought you were thirsty." He grabs my chips and eats one.

"Right. Right." I open a bottle of water, take a long swig, and offer it to him. I shove a handful of gummy bears into my mouth.

"Still want to have sex?" he asks.

I notice his erection has only deflated a little. He's still raring to go.

"Right. Sex. Let's go." I bring my snacks and water with me into the bedroom.

We settle ourselves in the middle of the bed, like always. I roll toward him and he faces me. We kiss and I taste a combination of smoke and tortilla chips on his tongue. He rolls us over so he's on top and slowly strokes me his fingers.

"I think you like giving blow jobs more than you admit. I can feel how excited you are," he whispers.

I am ridiculously horny today and feel like I've been ready since long before dinner. When he enters me, I moan and writhe beneath him, tilting my pelvis so he hits the right spot. We shift again and crunch the bag of chips beneath him. He reaches underneath and pulls out a chip. I lean forward and eat it.

"Eating during sex is new for us." He jokes. "You wanted new and exciting."

I spy a gummy bear on the pillow and offer it to him. It's orange. I hate the orange ones and he knows this.

He opens his mouth for me to toss it in. "So generous."

I actually forget that he's inside me for a moment until he thrusts again. "We're having sex right now," I say to let him know in case he's forgotten too.

"We are. Go us!" He pumps his fist in the air and grinds me against him.

We shift again and I nearly fall off the bed when we land too close to the edge. After some adjustments, we end up in the middle. I laugh when my head gets buried under the pillows.

It's the last thing I remember.

Ridiculously bright sunlight wakes me up. My head hangs off the edge of the bed and I have one leg dangling near the floor.

"What happened?" I mumble, trying to right myself enough to roll over.

The beautiful, snow white comforter and sheets are dotted with gummy bears and chip fragments. Ben's on his back, mouth open and snoring to the high heavens. I poke his chest and shake his shoulder.

"Wake up."

He grumbles and turns over. A few almonds are stuck in his hair.

"Wake up."

"What? Why is it so bright?" He burrows under the covers.

"It's morning. Weren't we having sex? That's the last thing I remember. We were having sex and now it's morning."

"We fell asleep."

"During sex?" I bury my head under my pillow. I lift just the edge to say, "We are the lamest people ever."

He laughs and pulls me into his arms. "I think we did fall asleep. Or during a position change, but we are not the lamest people ever. We can have more sex. We could have sex right now. And this afternoon. And tonight. Tomorrow, the next day, and so on until one of us dies."

I chuckle and turn in his arms. "You say the nicest, but most morbid things."

"It's the truth. We're the blessed ones, Jo. We found each other in college and still love each other. It's kind of a miracle if you think about it. We still want to be wild and adventurous with each other, even though we're both old."

"Again, best complimenter ever award goes to Benton Grant." I kiss the tip of his nose.

His eyes crinkle with happiness. "And the best wife and life partner ever goes to Josephine Grant."

"Now you're getting there. So this sex you were talking about?"

"Yes?" He kisses me, morning breath be damned.

"How about now?"

He kisses me again and we finish what we started last night. It doesn't involve ridiculously sexy but uncomfortable lingerie, or slightly medieval sex toys. No mind-altering substances either. Just us. Naked and loving each other.

It's pretty awesome sex.

For married people.

A NOTE FROM DAISY PRESCOTT

Thank you for reading this Modern Love Story Short.

I hope you enjoyed this glimpse into the lives of Ben and Jo Grant from *We Were Here* and *Geoducks Are for Lovers*. Chronologically, *Take for Granted* takes place after *Geoducks Are for Lovers*.

OUTDOOR SHOWER

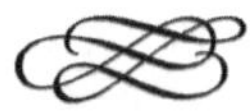

A WINGMEN SHORT

INTRODUCTION

Once upon a time, a blogger asked me to write a steamy scene with the hot next door neighbor in *Geoducks Are for Lovers*. Heather Maven and Love N Books were the catalyst for this scene, which launched the idea of *Ready to Fall*.

This short takes place after *Geoducks Are for Lovers* and before *Ready to Fall*.

THE INFAMOUS OUTDOOR SHOWER
SEX SCENE

"Are you sure we won't get caught?" she asked.

I turned around and we were eye to eye where she stood on the top step of my deck.

"Nothing to worry about. Maggie's out of town for the weekend. No one will interrupt us." I tugged her closer and leaned in for a kiss. She melted against my mouth, pressing her tits into my chest. I grabbed her by her thighs and lifted her up, and she wrapped her legs around my hips. I broke our kiss, and smiled.

"No more concerns?"

Her tongue in my mouth was my answer. I carefully stepped over the flowerbeds between my house and Maggie's. Kelly was wrapped tight around me, her legs a vice around my middle.

She bounced as I walked up the steps to Maggie's deck. Her hot center rubbed my erection and I moaned.

"Do I feel good, baby?" she asked.

"You feel so good. And you're going to feel even better when you're naked in the shower."

"I can't believe we're going to skinny dip in your neighbor's shower." She giggled and this time the rubbing wasn't from her bouncing.

"I think skinny dipping is only when you're swimming. Trust me, we're not going to be swimming in there."

"Not even the breast stroke?" She giggled again.

"Well, now that you mention it." I reached up and brushed my hand across her nipples, which hardened and perked under her shirt. I pinched one peak and her breath hitched. It was so hot the way she responded to my touch.

I tapped her leg with my left hand and she released her grip so I could slide her down my body, making sure she felt the full affect she had on me.

After opening the door to the shower, I turned on the hot water to let it warm up. When I faced her, Kelly was already tugging off her shoes and jeans.

"Eager much?" I teased, taking in the view of her long, bare legs.

She pointed at the noticeable bulge in my jeans. "I'm not the only one who looks eager. And I don't want to be waiting around naked out here in the open."

She emphasized these last words by pulling her shirt over her head. Her breasts looked amazing in her purple bra. They'd look even more amazing out of it.

As if she read my mind, she reached behind her back to unclasp her bra. I stopped her, wrapping my arms around her waist.

"Don't take away all my fun." I pretended to pout as I swiftly unhooked her bra with one hand and pulled it off. Her small breasts bounced slightly as they were freed from their confined space. Gorgeous.

Kelly wasn't shy. At all. She hadn't been in high school, and she wasn't now. I still couldn't believe my teenage crush stood in front of me. Naked. She quirked an eyebrow at me while I stared at her in the dusky light.

"Hello? How are you going to fuck me if you're fully clothed?"

"I'm getting there, babe. Don't rush me." I reached out and

squeezed her breasts, bending to lick one nipple before giving it a light nip with my teeth. She thrust her chest closer in response to my mouth, clearly liking the attention I was happy to give her.

I felt her hands at the button of my jeans as she quickly undid my fly before shoving the jeans open. Her hand was cool as it wrapped around my cock, making every teenage back of the car fantasy come true.

"Commando?"

"Figured why bother with you around. They'd just get tossed on a lamp or the floor again." I began unbuttoning my flannel shirt, only to have her hand stop me.

"Don't take away all my fun." She slowly eased each button through its hole, leaving a trail of kisses down my chest as she moved further and further south to where her other hand was stroking me.

"If you don't want anyone to see us, we better get in the shower." I stepped back into the enclosure and she followed, her hand still attached with a firm grip.

I moaned when the hot water hit me. Tipping my head back and closing my eyes, I let the water run over my head, down my face and chest. When I opened my eyes, Kelly was staring at my body.

"Like what you see?" I flexed my pecs to catch her attention.

She gave my cock a tug, and answered, "Like what I see and feel. Now move over and quit hogging the water."

I laughed, and stepped out of her way, watching as the water trailed down her body, before disappearing between her legs. I stepped behind her and pressed my body against her back. Reaching up, I grabbed her breasts and she tilted her head back to kiss me. My hips ground my erection into her lower back, just above the swell of her ass. Following the trails of water, I skimmed my hands lower. She spread her feet, widening the space between her legs for me as her arms wrapped around my neck. Her body echoed the movement of my thrusts.

Never losing contact with my mouth, she turned to face me. Hitching her leg, I wrapped her calf around my thigh, giving me access to more of her.

While my fingers explored her center, she tilted her head back under the water and I followed her. Water poured between us as we kissed, surrounded by the cool night air and the steam from the shower.

I could feel her body tensing and realizing she was close, I broke away from her lips and kneeled before her. Gently pushing her to lean against the shower wall, I kissed her thigh. Realizing where I was headed, Kelly placed her hand on my shoulder as I lifted her leg over my other one.

Water dripped from my soaked hair as I skimmed my beard up her inner thigh. The only sounds were of the spray of water hitting the teak decking and her increasingly loud moans. If she wasn't quiet, someone on the beach could easily hear us.

"Babe, you've got to keep quiet if you don't want an audience," I said, breaking away from her skin.

Kelly nodded and bit her knuckle when I returned to my business. I couldn't tell what was her own wetness and what was water as I licked, teased and nipped her. When she pulled my hair and ground her hips into my face, I added a finger, then two, finding that spot inside that made her clench and purr.

Her nails dug into my scalp and her leg tensed around my shoulder as I brought her to climax. God, I loved making a woman come.

Sitting back on my heels, I wiped my beard and pushed my hair back off my forehead before looking up into Kelly's dazed eyes.

"Come here," she whispered, reaching for my arm.

I did a quick rinse under the water before she spun me and pushed me against the wall. Her tongue found its way back into my mouth and her hands were everywhere at once—on my ass, my chest, my back and where I needed the most attention, my cock.

"Condom," I moaned, feeling myself getting harder in her hand.

"Where?"

"Back pocket," I replied as she reached under the door for my jeans. Tearing the packet with her teeth, she grinned at me.

Pushing her against the wall, I lifted her up, and she wrapped her legs around me again. With one fluid movement, I was inside her. With slow and steady thrusts, I fucked her against the wall as the water began to cool.

Biting my ear, she whispered, "You feel amazing, John. So fucking amazing."

Those words and the feel of her in my arms, her tits pressed against my chest and her ankles crossed behind my back, I was close to exploding. I swiveled my hips, needing to be as deep as possible. I could feel my orgasm moving down my spine as my movements became erratic.

"Fuck," I said with one final thrust, kissing her shoulder and neck to stifle the desire to shout.

Slowly coming down, I put her feet on the ground and braced my arms on the shower wall as my head swam from the force of my orgasm.

"Fuck. That was amazing," I said, stroking her face.

"You're amazing, baby," she said and turned off the now tepid shower.

Swallowing deep mouthfuls of air to calm my racing pulse, I got my bearings. I just had sex in Maggie's outdoor shower, but not with Maggie.

And I forgot to bring towels.

TAKE THE CAKE AND RUN

A WINGMEN SHORT

Originally published in the LOL Anthology with a "cake" theme, I knew I had to throw John Day, our strong and quiet lumberjack, into the midst of wedding planning shenanigans. The image of him in the pink bakery still makes me laugh.

Wedding planning.

Two words that strike fear in a six-foot-four alpha male.

Join John Day and his fiancé Diane in this laugh out loud Rom-Com short featuring everyone's favorite bearded hero, an over-the-top pink bakery, and things involving frosting you wouldn't want your future in-laws to know about.

Take the Cake and Run takes place chronologically after *Ready to Fall* and at the beginning of *Confessions of a Reformed Tom Cat.*

"You make the next shot, and I'll do it."

There was no way Diane would be able to get her last stripe around the eight ball and into the corner pocket.

Donnely scoffed from his perch on a nearby bar stool. "Diane, you've got this. I'd be happy to steady your hips while you take your shot, you know if you have to lean over the table or anything."

"Back off, D," I growled at him.

"We have a deal?" Diane asked, raising her eyebrow as she slowly bent from the waist over the pool table.

From my vantage point, I could see straight down her top to her pink bra. Donnely slowly strolled over to my side of the table, chalking up the end of his cue. Knowing full well what he was doing, I blocked his view with my body and gave him a dirty look. He tried to look innocent, but his swallowed-the-canary smile revealed his true thoughts.

His dimple didn't work on me the way it worked with women. I scowled at him.

"Take the shot, love." I crossed my arms and tightened my biceps, hoping to distract her. I knew she had a thing for my arms after the push-ups incident last year. This bet required playing dirty.

She winked at me and struck the cue ball, sending it into the far side of the table where it softly banked, slipped by the eight ball, and nudged her ball into the pocket before coming to rest on the edge of the green felt. If I were a cheating man, I would've blown on the ball to tip it into the pocket—it was that close to scratching.

"Damn." Donnely exhaled a long breath in a whistle and slapped my shoulder. "You need to learn not to bet against your woman, Day."

My shoulder hit his and he dropped the blue cube of chalk on the floor.

"Hey—" he said as he bent to find the cube.

I took the opportunity to saunter over to Diane. Slow, steady, with my gaze never wavering, my pace resembled a lion stalking its prey. Or maybe a panther.

Diane's smile faltered and a glimmer of fear creased her brow before she dashed around the table.

"John Day! A bet is a bet. You're not going back on your word, are you?"

When I caught up with her, my height towered over her smaller frame as I attempted to appear intimidating.

She stepped back and poked me in the chest with her index finger. "Stop with your big, bad lumberjack act."

Moving closer, I grabbed her finger and raised it to my lips to kiss the tip. Her lashes fluttered. I knew I had her. "Now, when have I ever given you reason to doubt me?" I gave her my crooked grin and then bit the corner of my mouth. I wanted to bite something else and she knew it.

With a quick tug, she pulled her finger from my grasp and

crossed her arms. Wrong move if she wanted me to focus on what she was saying.

Pink bra was my favorite and not because of the color. Her full boobs looked amazing peeking out from her plaid shirt. I wondered how strong those buttons were and how hard I'd have to bite to rip them off with my teeth. Thoughts of bending her over the pool table flickered through my mind. If only Donnely and Olaf weren't here. *Maybe O would let me lock up the bar tonight.*

Donnely's cough snapped me out of my thoughts about thread strength and pool table height. My eyes focused and I realized I was staring at Diane's chest while the two of them stared at me. Well, Donnely kept sneaking glances at the same spot that held my attention.

"Dude, show your fiancé some respect. Eyes above the collar, Day."

I wanted to wipe the smirk off his face. "Don't you have a date or some other place else to be right now?"

He tilted his head and glanced at the clock above the bar. "Nah. It's Thursday. We always play pool on Thursdays at the Dog House."

Something about his answer and the way he frowned at the clock told me there was more to his night, but there was no way I would push him.

Tom and I were friends, not sisters.

One awkward conversation about dating and women outside this very bar last year was enough to last us for a while. Or forever.

The object of that conversation stepped closer to me and wrapped her arms around my hips. I tugged her in close with one arm and placed my pool cue on the table.

Softly, so only she could hear, I whispered near the top of her head, "You know I'll do anything you want, but don't ruin my manly man image in front of the guys."

Her arms tightened around me and she leaned back. "I think it was Donnely who first proclaimed you whipped. Not news to him."

"Yeah, but Olaf still thinks I'm a real ladies' man." I nodded my head in the direction of the bartender, who was carefully counting out the cash drawer. The old salt was going deaf so I hadn't bothered lowering my voice.

"No, I don't. You're about as smitten as a man can be and still pee standing up," Olaf scoffed without turning around.

D snorted into the dregs of his pint glass.

"Laugh all you want Donnely. You'll be next." I glowered at him and he stopped.

Confirmed bachelor and nicknamed Tom Cat, Donnely falling in love was as about as likely as a King salmon jumping on your line, but not as improbable as a lumberjack wearing women's underwear. Tom's definition of dating meant breakfast the morning after and maybe a repeat or two if he really enjoyed himself.

Not that long ago I was his wingman, the dark to his light. Being the better looking of the two of us, I probably made his life easier after I fell for this beautiful, brown-eyed girl.

Whipped, smitten, whatever they wanted to tease me with, I didn't care. I nearly lost this woman once due to idiocy, I wasn't going to let a few insults bug me.

She laughed and kissed my neck between my beard and the collar of my T-shirt. "Let's get you home before you punch your best friend. If you do that, who will be your best man?"

Right. The wedding.

I, John Day, was getting married. Thirty-three years as a bachelor and then Diane stumbled into my life. After turning down my offer of a trip to the Hitching Post in Idaho back when I proposed in February, Diane agreed to a small island wedding in May. Neither of us wanted anything fancy, and to be honest, I was still hoping to convince her to elope.

So far no luck.

Instead, my lackluster pool skills and inability to turn down a bet meant I was going to some fancy bakery over in Seattle to taste wedding cake.

It had better not be one of those over-the-top places all in pink.

CHAPTER 2

The following weekend, I parked my truck in front of Sweet Endings Cakes in Bellevue. Pink and white striped awnings did not bode well for this going anything but disastrous.

"Stop grumbling and acting like you're being tortured." Diane hopped down from the truck. "You get to eat cake. Lots of cake. You like cake."

I grumbled some more. "I like my aunt's chocolate cake. Can't we just have that?" I stared through the window. "If there's lace and tiny plates, I'm out of here. Nothing froufy."

"Focus on the cake, and you'll be fine." She gave my arm a gentle shove.

Taking the hint, I opened the door. A wave of butter and sugar scented air hit me squarely in the face. *Okay, maybe this wouldn't be terrible.*

As I inhaled, my attention caught on a wall covered in pink flowers. Row after row of frilly, frou-frou girly cupcakes and little miniature cakes in pinks and purples sat on lace circles inside glass cases. I coughed and gave Diane a pointed look.

"Buttercream" she whispered.

We weren't the only people in the bakery. A few pairs of women, mostly resembling mothers and daughters, perched at tiny tables on tiny, delicate chairs that looked like they were made of pipe-cleaners.

Feeling like a bull in a bakery, I attempted to make my six foot four frame smaller by slouching and stepping closer to the door. I tugged at my beard and scratched the back of my neck. Without meaning to, my ass hit a small bookcase and sent it wobbling.

"Oh shit." I settled the shelves and the books on the top. I felt several pairs of female eyes focus on me. "Shit, sorry for swearing."

All heads turned and I felt the weight of a thousand staring eyes on me. Okay, so it was more like six, but they were judgmental looks.

Diane grabbed my hand and laced her fingers with mine. "What is wrong with you?"

I was about to say my balls were shrinking from all the pink in the room, when a woman resembling Mrs. Doubtfire came through a pair of swinging doors at the back of the space. She smiled at the other ladies, checking in and chatting with them as she walked through the bakery.

"You must be Diane and John. I'm Cassandra." She shook Diane's hand. Her scent of sugar and spice enveloped us a few seconds later.

I wondered if this was how the witch smelled in Hansel and Gretel. Probably.

After she seated us and promised to return with the samples, Diane stroked my thigh. "Quit grinding your teeth. I can see your jaw ticking and it's beginning to look painful."

I unlocked my jaw, rolled my shoulders, and placed my hand over hers. Normally her hand on my thigh would get the blood flowing, but sitting on a delicate white chair in Barbie's Dream Bakery had destroyed my libido. Diane's hand swept higher and she let her nails scrape along the denim covering my thigh.

Okay, maybe my libido wasn't completely DOA. Her hand moved toward my fly and I didn't stop her. Less blood in my brain would make this experience easier.

A burst of cinnamon and sugar announced the return of our hostess-baker-lady-witch. She set a huge tray on the table. Rows of small bites of cakes, frostings, sauces, a few cupcakes, and cookies filled every inch of the surface.

I eyed the chocolate frosting as Diane and Cassandra chatted about foundations, tiers, shape, and layers. For all I knew, they were building a house together.

"John?"

I broke off my staring contest with the cakes and met Diane's warm brown eyes.

"What do you think?" she asked.

I blinked at her.

"You weren't listening, were you?"

"Nope." I shrugged, feeling a little embarrassed, but not really caring, because, cake.

"We probably should have discussed all this before you put the cake samples out." Diane apologized, laughing.

"Most men don't care about the cake. They're more focused on the honeymoon." Cassandra's face hid nothing. Sex. Men were more focused on sex, her eyes said.

True.

At least we agreed about that.

"John has a sweet tooth about a mile long. I thought it would be fun to decide together. Plus, my mother is on the other side of the country."

"Isn't that sweet. Well, I'll leave you to it." Cassandra's eyes settled briefly on the spot where Diane's hand rested on my thigh before she walked away.

"Shall we?" Diane's hand squeezed my thigh.

I swallowed thickly, partly due to the thought of desecrating the pink palace by having my way with her under her skirt and partly due to the huge platter of cake in front of us.

When I didn't respond, Diane pinched my skin through the denim.

"Ouch!" I swatted her hand away. Pain near that part of my body wasn't a good thing.

"Let's start." She pointed at the cupcakes and other stuff. Grabbing a fork, she gestured to the small cakes first. "Pick a cake, frosting and sauce, put them all on your fork and taste. That's how we'll decide what combination we like best."

"I like chocolate with chocolate frosting."

She stuck out her tongue at me, but loaded a fork with chocolate cake, chocolate sauce and chocolate frosting.

"Here." She held the fork near my mouth.

"Are you going to feed me?"

"If you're going to continue to act like a giant bearded toddler about being here, yes."

"Make the airplane noises." I gave her my best clothing incinerating smile, and chuckled.

She shoved the forkful of food into my mouth.

Holy amazing … damn.

"This is mmamazing," I said through a mouthful of the best thing I'd ever had in my mouth.

I licked my lips to remove any extra frosting.

"You have it in your beard." Diane's eyes focused on my mouth.

I used the pad of my thumb to rub a spot near my mouth and then sucked off the chocolate I found there. "Good?"

Her eyes glazed over. I knew that look. It took me a while to recognize it when we first met, but now there was no mistaking the lust that shone in her eyes. "Diane?"

She inhaled and met my gaze. "What?"

"Cake?" I put some white cake, red glaze and chocolate frosting on my fork.

Her full lips opened and her pink tongue peeked out to lick a drop of sauce before it fell. Her stare never left my eyes.

I gulped when she wrapped her lips around the soft cake and pulled back, wiping the fork clean. Her moan was loud and not at all appropriate for a bakery.

Shit.

I needed Divine intervention to make it out of this pink nightmare alive, so I said a little prayer.

Lord, please keep me from getting a boner and tipping over this doll table with my dick.

Appreciate it, thanks.

Closing my eyes, I inhaled and thought about soccer.

"You have to try this one." She held a forkful of the same combination near my face.

No doubt about it, it was incredible. The red sauce tasted like raspberries.

Sometimes Diane smelled and tasted like raspberries, right between her breasts, especially in the summer

Damn. Not helping. I thought about Pelé.

"Can we get this to go?"

"You want to leave already? But we haven't tried everything yet." Her lips turned down in a frown.

"I'll create a distraction and you run out to the truck. Or I'll walk out first and meet you out back with the engine running." I licked raspberry flavored sauce from the corner of my lip. I suspected she had intentionally missed my open mouth again.

She shook her head at me. "Stop doing that," she whispered. "Those women are staring at you."

"What?" I turned in my seat and caught both women at the next table staring.

"You know what. The thing with the tongue and the frosting. You're putting on a floor show." Diane's cheeks were flushed and her eyes held a familiar sparkle.

"This?" I asked, lifting a blob of frosting with my forefinger and bringing it to her lips. She sucked on the tip like I knew she would. "Yeah, I'm not the only one torturing someone at this table."

"Truce?" She brushed the toe of her shoe across my shin.

"Truce." I licked my bottom lip. "For now."

She exhaled an unsteady breath. "Let's try the red velvet."

We tasted the rest of the cakes and frostings, and only once did I reach over to lick frosting from her cheek. I sucked at following truces when it came to her. Why should I deny myself something I wanted?

Everything tasted delicious except the weird mango puree the color of boxed mac and cheese. Cassandra and her sweet fragrance returned. She clucked and cooed over us while talking about a cake per guest ratio.

While studying the bakery and other patrons, I zoned out only to realize one of the mothers in a pink fuzzy sweat suit was staring back at me. She winked, lifted her fork, and licked the underside of it.

What the hell?

I quickly glanced somewhere else, anywhere else. Salvation: bathroom sign.

"I'll be right back." I stood and my full height felt even more ridiculous in this space.

The bathroom was not meant for men. No urinal. Although if there was one, I bet the urinal cake would have been pink. Flowers, cupcakes, and pink decorated every surface, including the toilet. Tiny donuts and cupcakes danced around the seat. I closed my eyes and thought about fishing and football.

Hell, I was comfortable living with a woman and all of the girl shit that came with it, but this was man-hell. Pink man-hell.

My hands even smelled like cupcakes when I finished up. Cassandra must bathe in the hand soap.

Diane and I were going to need to stop at Ivar's for a beer

before taking the ferry back to the island. Maybe some college basketball would be on TV in the bar.

"Ready?" I asked when I returned.

"Cassandra's just boxing up a few things for us."

"You're the best." I leaned down to kiss the top of her head.

Back in the truck, I inhaled the scent of work: pine, gasoline and yeah, maybe some sweat. I scratched my beard on my chin and smiled. "You owe me."

"I totally do. I had no idea it would be so prissy." She reached over and squeezed my arm. "However can I make it up to you?"

From the corner of my eye, I saw her batting her lashes at me. "I'm sure you'll think of something." My hand rested on top of two small boxes sitting between us on the bench seat.

The boxes were pink.

Of course.

CHAPTER 3

A slim, dark moon hung low outside and the only light in the house came from the fridge. I stood in front of it in my boxers, trying to figure out something to eat. I poked through several foil wrapped leftovers inside: salmon steaks, crab cakes, some noodle casserole, and a half-eaten pork chop. I stuck the bone of the chop in my mouth and grabbed the bowl of noodles, and added a hunk of cheese on top. Not bad for a snack. Before closing the door, a pair of pink boxes on the counter caught my eye.

Gnawing on the chop, I opened the top box and peered inside.

Cupcakes.

I glanced over my shoulder and listened for sounds upstairs to make sure I wouldn't get caught.

Nothing.

Something bumped my leg and I dropped the bowl of noodles on the floor where it clattered and spilled its contents.

Babe's long tail thumped against the cabinet doors.

Damn dog.

At least I hadn't squealed like a girl.

Before I could say anything, he gobbled a big pile of casserole.

"No," I scolded him.

He looked up at me and took another bite before sitting down. "Stay."

He cocked his head and his tail whacked the floor. I swear he licked his lips, too.

I turned on the under cabinet lights and then grabbed some paper towels to clean up the mess. Bending over, I wiped up the noodles.

"Midnight snack?" Diane leaned in the doorway behind me.

"Yeah. I couldn't sleep and thought I'd watch some soccer." I stood and noticed she was wearing one of my flannel shirts. Her hair was all messed up and she looked sleepy and beautiful, and her arms were crossed.

Uh oh.

She stepped closer and bit into the pork chop still in my hand. "With dessert?"

The lid to the bakery box stood open.

Busted.

"Were they off limits?' I asked.

"Not exactly, but I thought we could, um—" She paused. "—eat them together."

So much could be said within a single pause.

"Together?" I held out the pork chop for her to take another bite.

"Mmm hmm." She licked her lips and chewing.

"What did you have in mind?" I picked up the box and put it on the island between us.

She removed the chop from my fingers and set it on the counter before opening the box. "Oh, I don't know."

"Love?"

Her eyes met mine.

"I'm getting the feeling you meant something specific."

She stared at the frosting.

I waited.

Not meeting my eyes, she explained, "When we were at the bakery, I had this fantasy."

"Fantasy?"

"Involving you, me, and some frosting."

"Food fantasy?"

She nodded.

I moved closer and caged her against the island with my arms. "Tell me more."

"That's about it. All that licking and sweet frosting earlier did something to me."

"I'd like to do something to you." I lifted her up to the counter next to the box.

"All those women were lusting after you."

"So?" I nuzzled her neck.

"I had this overwhelming urge to sit on your lap and make out with you so they'd stop trying to eat you with their eyes."

My woman was jealous. I wrapped my arms around her and pulled her to the edge of the counter. "Jealous? Of the pink fuzzy woman?"

"I saw what she did with her fork. It was pornographic."

I chuckled and kissed the spot at the corner of her jaw that always made her squirm. "Yeah, that was weird, but you know you have nothing to worry about. No cougar, no matter how hot her sweatsuit is, will ever lure me away from you. Ever." I stared into her beautiful eyes.

"I know, I know, but I still wanted to mark you as mine."

"You're wearing my ring."

I let my gaze rest on her left finger on the counter where my mom's ring sparkled. It has only been two months since I proposed, but I doubted I'd ever stop feeling my heart flip over every time I saw it on her hand.

Her arms draped around my neck and she pulled me down to her, kissing me while she wrapped her legs around my waist.

"You being jealous is all kinds of hot, in case you were

wondering." I returned her kiss, letting my tongue find hers. Her boobs pressed against my chest and my hands wandered between us to cup them through my shirt. "I love you in my shirt."

She hummed in contentment when my thumbs swept across her nipples. Her hips rocked forward to brush against the front of my boxers. Her warm heat transferred to my dick.

I reluctantly pulled back from her lips. "So about this fantasy of yours? I squished my index finger into a cupcake and swept a line of pink frosting over her cheek.

She squirmed and giggled. "John ..."

"What? This is your fantasy. Or was frosting on your face not what you were thinking?" Another swipe of frosting found its way onto her skin, this time on her exposed collarbone.

Her hand moved to wipe the frosting from her cheek, but I stopped her. "No, let me."

I slowly, carefully, and maybe torturously, licked the sweet, sticky substance from her skin. Leaning back, I met her stare, and then licked my lips. "Delicious. But we're going to need to lose the shirt."

My shirt fell to the floor in a blur of movement. I blinked, taking in naked Diane on the counter.

This wouldn't be the first time we had sex in this kitchen. My mind flashed back to pancakes, and more importantly, maple syrup, on this very island. I felt myself harden at the memory.

Diane's finger dipped into the frosting and she traced a circle with it on my bicep, before shadowing the line with her tongue. Her warm mouth contrasted with the cool air she breathed on my skin after, creating goose-flesh on my arm. I reacted by flexing my hips into her center.

Her gasp let me know she felt my tip brush across her. Quickly after, her hands shoved my boxers down my legs. She used her feet to push them to the floor.

"Lean back," I told her.

She followed my instructions and lay there, beautifully exposed to me.

"So beautiful." I kissed a line from the hollow of her collarbones down to her navel, but didn't go any further south, knowing she was on the verge of begging me.

Instead, I peered inside the box and found a small container of red syrup. I prayed it was raspberry sauce when I opened it. The scent of ripe berries enveloped me as I drizzled some over her belly and tits. Thick, red dots covered her nipples and slowly slid down over the slope of her breast to drip on her skin below.

I poked out my tongue to catch a drop and then kissed her, her own taste mixing with the berries.

Damn, I loved the way she tasted.

Her hands wandered over my arms and chest. She reached over for the frosting and circled her boobs with chocolate.

"You're going to kill me." I leaned down and licked her skin clean. I sucked on her nipples a little harder than was nice, but I wanted to make sure they were clean.

"Oww... mmm," Diane moaned and turned her head. Another finger-full of frosting found its way onto my skin, this time on my neck.

I cocked my head to allow her access to lick it off. She bit my ear lobe before lying back down.

Two could play at the teasing game.

I stepped back from the counter's edge and slid my hands down her thighs. Grabbing the sauce, I poured a thin line from one knee to the other, pausing to let some pool between her legs. Starting at her right knee, I licked up the sauce, letting my beard drag along her skin where my tongue had just been. I had to use my hands to still her squirming as I tortured her.

I let my breath hover over her center but didn't lick up the sauce there before I moved to the other leg and my sticky path to her knee.

"John ..." Diane's voice was tense, almost annoyed.

I smiled into her thigh to hide my amusement. I knew she'd get me back, but this was too much fun to stop.

When I reached her knee, I lifted up her leg and rested her calf on my shoulder. Her eyes slowly opened and she glared at me. Or tried to glare. The lust and need I saw there clouded out her pretend anger. I nipped her calf and bent forward to finish the job.

Every inch between her thighs was covered in raspberry sauce, and it pooled on the counter beneath her. This would be messy.

Not that I complained.

I licked and sucked, covering my beard in sweet, sticky raspberry-flavored Diane. I braced her other leg on my shoulder and wrapped my hands under her butt and around her hips.

As she began to buck against my tongue, I found the spot inside that would push her over the edge. Two fingers slightly curled were all it took for her to lose herself. The taste of Diane combined with berries became my new favorite flavor.

I kept lapping at her until her hands tugging on my hair stilled me.

I stood and grinned at her.

"You are a fine mess, Day." She crooked her finger at me and I bent to kiss her.

"Yeah?" I dragged a finger through the mess I had just made on her. "So are you." I sucked on my finger before kissing her again.

She giggled. "You're all sticky, and your beard smells of sex and berries."

"I may never wash my face again." I licked the corner of my mouth.

"My turn." She hopped off the counter. With a devilish gleam in her eye, she scooped up all the chocolate frosting from a cupcake and reached for my dick. Cool, smooth icing coated me as she moved her hand from the base to tip.

"This is a first."

"What?"

"Frosting hand job. Where were you in junior high?"

"Girls were giving you hand jobs in junior high?"

"Not really, and never with frosting."

Her eyebrow raised in question.

I shrugged. "Late bloomer, remember? Scrawny kid who lived and breathed soccer? The Nineties weren't my best decade."

She bent at the waist to lick me. "Nothing scrawny about you now."

That was the last thing she said for a while.

Hard to talk with a mouthful of frosting.

Closing my eyes, I leaned against the counter as she used her mouth to remove every trace of frosting. Her tongue ran up the underside and I jerked in response. My hand on the counter knocked the box onto the floor, but I couldn't care less.

If I didn't stop her soon, I'd finish in her mouth.

Not tonight. I had other plans.

My hand resting on her cheek paused her movements. Her eyes blinked open and met mine. Nothing could be hotter than seeing her from this angle. She slowly dragged her lips over the tip and held me in her hand. Her eyes held a silent question.

"I'm close and you need to stop."

Her lips rose in a knowing smile. "Where do you want me?"

"Floor," I grunted out when her hand squeezed me.

She tumbled backward and I followed, landing between her thighs. Something sticky pressed into my knee and she still had sauce on her hips.

"We're a mess," she said between kisses.

"This isn't going to be slow and sweet." I nipped her shoulder.

A giggle followed her moan. "Pun intended?"

"No." I lined up with her and thrust inside in one movement. "I was thinking hard and fast."

"Mmm, my favorite."

She rolled on top and I held onto her hips as she rode me. Nothing sweet about her now.

I flipped us back over and kneeled, lifting her hips with me. That did it. I was so deep in this position; my vision started to darken in the corners, and a familiar building feeling pushed me toward the point-of-no-return.

With a low growl, I thrust and then stilled as I came inside her. Damn.

We lay sprawled out on the kitchen floor for a few minutes in the quiet. She had frosting in her hair and I still had sauce in my beard. Cake crumbs laid on her naked chest from where she nibbled on a squashed cupcake. I pressed a finger into one of the chocolate crumbs and licked it off. The counter and floor were both covered in our mess. Even my shirt had frosting on it where it lay on the floor next to my boxers.

"Who knew cake could be so much fun?" I asked.

"See? You were so cranky about Sweet Endings. I knew the cake would change your mind."

"I don't think you naked with frosting in your hair and covered in raspberry sauce were what Cassandra had in mind when she opened the pink palace of cake."

Her hand landed on my shoulder with a thwack. "John Day!"

"What?" I rubbed my shoulder. She hit like a boy.

"That sweet woman didn't name her bakery after some sort of sex euphemism."

"Are you sure? It's always the ones in the dumpy cardigans who turn out to be the biggest perverts. At least in my experience." I dodged her hand and pulled her onto my lap.

"We burned that sweater, remember?" Her hands tugged at my beard at the corner of my jaw.

"Still doesn't change the fact that inside all that wool was the naked girl sitting in my lap right now."

She ground her hips into mine, stirring me back to life. I knew she felt me getting hard beneath her by the way her eyes widened.

"And you, Mr. Day, are a horn-dog in flannel clothing."

"Did you just call me a horn-dog?"

"Yep. Seemed to fit the whole frosting hand-job conversation from earlier."

"Can't argue with that logic. Speaking of flannel, we should have a plaid cake."

"Plaid?"

"Yeah, like my shirt. Better than pink any day."

"Maybe for the groom's cake?"

"I get my own cake? Do I have to share it? Like with the guests? Or just the best man? 'Cause I'm not sure I'd want to give Donnely any. I mean, it's not the groomsmen cake." This sounded like a great idea to me.

"John?"

"Yes, Diane?"

"Let's get married."

I grinned at her and kissed her nose. "Already doing that." I picked up a piece of red velvet cake from the crushed box on the floor. "Remember? Wedding cake tasting is how we ended up here."

"No, I mean, now."

"Right now?" I wiped off a spot of chocolate on her cheek and held it up to her.

She sucked on my finger. "No, not this minute. Just soon. Soon and no fancy Seattle wedding cakes. We can do it on the beach—"

"We've already done it on the beach. A few times, if I remember correctly. That time by the beach fire. Christening our new outdoor shower." I interrupted her. I couldn't help myself.

"You know what I mean. I never wanted fancy or big."

I lifted my eyebrows and my beard twitched.

"Stop! I'm not talking about your dick or having sex with you." Exasperated, she wove her fingers into my hair and pulled my head back.

"Okay, I'll focus. But you get any feistier and I won't be able to concentrate."

She growled and I kissed her. A few minutes later she was panting, but no longer frustrated with me.

"Can we have my aunt's chocolate cake?"

"Yes, I was going to ask her to make it for us anyway."

I frowned at her. "So today was for?"

She pressed her lips together and looked over my shoulder. I grabbed her ass and squeezed to get her attention.

"I heard their cakes were amazing and wanted to try them. And you like cake. So it seemed like a win-win for everyone."

"Diane…"

"You can't be mad. You got cake, and frosting. And a frosting hand-job." She squirmed off of my lap before I could catch her.

"I had to play the Beast in a tiny pink theater production of Beauty and the Beast today for your amusement?" I stalked her around the counter. Naked or not, covered in sauce, frosting, and cake crumbs, she was still the most beautiful woman I'd ever seen.

How she was mine and wanting to be my wife, I wasn't going to question. All that being said, she was still in trouble.

I paused and she scampered toward the hall.

"Oh, you better run, Mrs. Day." I counted to ten to give her a head-start up the stairs. When I heard her turn on the shower, I pounded up the stairs after her.

I loved shower sex even more than cake.

CHAPTER 4

One thing about the Sweet Endings experience, both the bakery and what happened in our kitchen, was I could never look at red velvet cake or raspberry sauce the same way again.

Thursday night back at the Dog House it was just Donnely and I playing pool. Diane had a late Pilates client and promised to meet us after. Her studio was only two blocks away in Langley's small downtown. I offered to meet her and walk her back, but she insisted she'd be fine walking at night. It wasn't like we lived in the city. Hell, the Dog House was the only real tavern in this four street town.

Donnely racked up the balls and then took solids. "How'd the wedding planning go? You get your balls monogrammed yet?"

I ignored him and took my shot.

"I'm taking your silence as a yes. Damn, I can't believe in a year you've gone from bachelor to married."

"We're not married yet."

"Having cold feet?"

"Not at all. I would've kept driving over the pass to the

Hitching Post in Idaho if she said yes. It's the wedding I'm not looking forward to. All the fuss."

"Hey, didn't you get free cake out of the deal last weekend? Can I fake being engaged and go get free shit?"

Pink dots flashed in my peripheral vision like some sort of post-traumatic stress hallucination. "Trust me, you'd never survive the process. Tom Cats can't be domesticated."

Donnely frowned. "You never know."

"That'll be the day." I laughed.

When he didn't joke back, I raised my eyebrow at him, but he lined up his shot and refused to look at me. I shrugged it off. He'd tell me what was going on when he was ready.

"The free cake was pretty amazing, but I swear the woman and the place were the creepiest things you've ever seen." I told him about the dancing cakes on the toilet.

We laughed about the cougar and the fork.

"I've been with an older woman before." Tom confessed.

"Just one?"

"I mean like mid-forties."

"And?"

"She was wild in bed. Totally hot." He sipped his beer and paused in memory. "I would have gone out with her again."

"Why didn't you?"

"When I left in the morning I realized I'd also slept with her daughter." He shuddered. "That was weird. I mean, she didn't even look that old. Must have been a teen mom or something."

I shook my head. "Tom."

"Don't even start. I know."

If I even needed a reminder how lucky I was to have found Diane and be loved by her, this conversation was it.

Mother and daughter? That crossed a line somewhere into manwhore. Tom was a good guy.

"Hey, I could always set you up with one of Diane's friends if you—"

"No way! Not the married friend hook-up. My sisters have pulled that shit on me for years. Single or suddenly divorced and looking to play, but then complain when I won't settle down. Been there and done that."

I lifted my hands up palms facing him. "Okay, okay."

We continued our game. Tom swept the table on his next turn while I nursed our pitcher of beer.

Any time someone walked by or entered the tavern's double doors, my head swung around to see if it was Diane.

I glanced at the clock, realizing Diane would only be finishing with her client now. I resisted the temptation to jog over to the studio to meet her at the door.

A few minutes later, the doors swung open and a familiar scent of raspberries wafted toward me. She pulled off her grey knitted hat and shook out her long hair. Even in her workout clothes, my woman was a vision.

"Hi, Donnely." She greeted Tom with a hug, and then waved to Olaf at the bar before walking over to me. "Hi, honey."

She stood on her tiptoes and I leaned down to kiss her. There was something sweet on her lips. I licked my bottom lip to taste it.

"Why do you taste so amazing?" I kissed her again before she could answer. I couldn't figure out the flavor, but I was willing to keep kissing her to find out.

"Ahem, you two can take that home if you keep at it. This is a family place," Olaf scolded us from behind the bar.

Diane stepped away from me to look around the room. Peter sat at the end of the bar with Lester, and both looked up at the mention of family before returning to their discussion of baseball.

I scratched my beard and chuckled. "Okay, O, we get it."

Diane set down a white box on the thin ledge that ran behind the stools near the pool table before taking off her coat.

"What's in the box?" I walked over to have a look.

"Nothing." She swatted my hand away and moved the box under her coat.

"Diane? What's in the box?"

She blushed and poured herself a glass of beer. "It's something a client brought me."

"Okay, that was vague."

"Can I look?" Donnely asked.

He reached for the box, but Diane spun around and lunged in front of him to protect it.

"Wow. It must be dirty with the way you're blushing. Sex toys? Kinky stuff to keep things interesting?" He wiggled his eyebrows and gave her his best attempt at a seductive grin.

"Shut it, D." I wrapped my arm around her shoulders and leaned down to whisper in her ear. "So what is it? And why are your clients bringing you kinky shit?"

"Stop it. It's not kinky. At all. You two have the dirtiest minds." With an exasperated sigh, she opened the box.

Tom and I peered inside like two kids allowed to peek at their Christmas presents.

"It's cupcakes." He sounded disappointed. "And not even chocolate."

Inside the box sat four cupcakes and a small container of raspberry sauce. That's what I'd tasted on Diane's lips—vanilla frosting. My body reacted like one of Pavlov's dogs. Heat raced through my veins and blood headed south.

Great.

Any time I had dessert now, I'd be at risk of sporting.

Diane leaned into me, bringing me back into the moment. "You need some help with that wood in your pants?"

"You're an evil minx."

"I told you not to open the box, but you didn't listen. Had to open it, didn't you?"

"Let's go," I growled into her ear.

"But I just got here and I haven't even played a game, or finished my beer—"

I cut her off by grabbing her hand and the cake box, tugging her toward the door.

"Sorry to play and run, Donnely, but we need to go."

"But my coat—" Diane wiggled out of my grip and retrieved her stuff while I waited by the door.

Donnely stood by the pool table and grinned. He mouthed "whipped" at me.

I flipped him the bird.

I heard him say "Lucky bastard" as I pulled Diane out into the night. I couldn't get her home soon enough.

"How are we going to have cake at the wedding if this is how you react now every time you see frosting?" She giggled as she jogged to keep up with me back to the truck.

I swung her around so her back rested against the truck door and kissed her, tasting vanilla and pure Diane. "I've decided we should have pie."

TAKE IT EASY

A WINGMEN SHORT

INTRODUCTION

First published in Red Hot Candy, this silly short captures the friendship between John and Tom as they adjust from being solo wingmen to their new lives with Diane and Hailey. Summers in the Pacific Northwest are my favorite.

When Diane and Hailey join John and Tom for a weekend in the San Juan Islands, it won't be the typical guys' camping trip the best friends and former wingmen are used to having.

Two couples, four friends in the woods… one crazy night.

Take it Easy takes place chronologically after *Ready to Fall* and *Confessions of a Reformed Tom Cat* . It's better enjoyed after reading *Take the Cake and Run*

I sat on the tailgate of John's truck, watching the ferry wake churn the dark water into white froth. The ship's engines hummed as we made our way north. My faded Mariners' cap blocked the bright August glare from my face. The summer sun warmed my bare arms and legs despite the wind. A few seagulls rode the air currents above the wake, carefree.

Beside me, Hailey slowly swung her feet, her long tanned legs exposed below shorts that covered little more than her ass. I liked her ass and legs. A feral part of me wanted her to wear one of those long skirts to keep other men from checking out my girlfriend.

Yeah, the Tom Cat found himself a girlfriend.

She was more than that, though. Someday she'd be a Donnely, too.

Not this summer, though. John went and got himself hitched and that was enough wedding stuff for one year.

I trailed my fingers up Hailey's leg, causing her to squirm.

"Don't start anything you're not willing to finish," she whispered. Her eyes were hidden by sunglasses, but I knew from the tone of her voice, she meant it.

"Ever had sex on a ferry?" I snuck a fingertip between the edge of her shorts and her inner thigh.

"No, and I'm not about to on a full, Friday afternoon boat headed for the San Juans."

"That's not a 'never.' I'll keep those details in mind on one of those late night winter crossings where we're one of a handful of cars and everyone else is trying to stay warm upstairs." I nipped the skin of her shoulder. "Thanks for clarifying."

"Stop teasing, Thor." She turned her head and smiled.

I scratched the scruff on my cheek. I'd impulsively shaved off my beard a few weeks ago. Hailey had nicknamed me Thor. I was pretty sure it was a compliment.

John and his wife Diane strolled over to us, holding sodas from the galley.

Wife. I couldn't stop calling her that. So weird to think my best friend was married. It had only been a month or so since the lumberjack tied the knot and I gave the greatest best man speech ever. I mean, how many toasts mentioned both geoducks *and* wood jokes yet were tasteful enough to avoid getting punched or embarrassing the bride? Only mine. Without a doubt, I put the "best" in best man.

"Hey, Mrs. Day, you excited to go camping?"

Diane glanced up at John. "I thought we were staying in a cabin?"

"You didn't tell her we're doing pack-in/pack-out tent camping with a ten mile, uphill hike to the spot? Whoa, man. You gotta give girls a heads-up on this stuff." I stared at John, holding back my smile by biting my cheek.

"Tom Clifford, enough of your teasing." Hailey pinched my bicep muscle in her version of a Vulcan grip.

"Ouch!" I yelped and scooted away from her.

"I know he's teasing. I booked the cabin myself. Two bedrooms, two baths, porch, firepit next to the lake. That's about as close to sleeping on the ground as I'll get."

"You didn't mind that time we went to South Whidbey State Park." John wrapped his big arm around her.

Diane's cheeks reddened and she took a long sip through her straw. John chewed on a handful of corn nuts.

Okay, then. Clearly someone had some camping lovins in the woods. Wasn't going to ask for details.

"What's the plan for the weekend?" Hailey asked, ignoring the awkward moment John had created.

"Nothing. I plan to do nothing but take it easy. Sleep in. Fish. Eat. Have sex," I answered.

Everyone laughed.

"What? She asked." I took off my cap and ran my fingers through my hair. It was long enough to start curling. Hailey liked it longer. Said it gave her something to hold onto, so I'd let it grow.

"Sounds like a good plan to me." John backed me up.

"All but the fishing works for me," Diane added. "We'll nap while you guys go hunt food."

"You make us sound like cavemen," I said.

The girls exchanged glances and laughed.

"If the name fits, Thor." Hailey teased and jumped off the tailgate.

"Thor definitely suits him. He's definitely an angry Norse god or long, lost Hemsworth brother." Diane high-fived Hailey.

"It's perfect, isn't it?" she replied, a smug smile on her face.

John took Hailey's spot next to me as the girls continued to congratulate themselves on their cleverness. With their similar brown hair, they could be sisters. Diane was shorter and curvier while Hailey had that Amazon look, all long legs and kickass…

"Are we sure this is a good idea?" he asked, keeping his eyes on Diane.

"Letting them feel smug? Probably not, but what can it hurt? They already know they have all the power."

He smiled and bowed his head. "Ain't that the truth. I meant taking them out to Friday Harbor with us."

"Can't be worse than camping with the Kelso brothers."

"Right. Never doing that again."

Plus, I had a plan for some fun that might return some of our guy power. I hadn't mentioned it to John yet, but it involved a campfire and snipes.

CHAPTER 2

"*H*ow is it possible you've never been snipe hunting, Diane? You have brothers, don't you?" I stretched my legs toward the fire ring, extinguishing a bright red ember with the toe of my boot.

Hailey rested her head against my shoulder. Her short nails scratched a figure eight pattern on my bicep through the thin material of my flannel shirt. Across from us sat John and Diane. Going on ten o'clock, the sky had finally darkened about an hour ago after a long Friday afternoon of doing nothing. A few yards away, the lake barely made waves at the shore. The fire crackled and popped, and the only sound besides us was an occasional owl or muffled voice in the distance. Our cabin was at the end of a road, with only woods behind us. I inhaled the smell of smoke and pine trees.

"What's a snipe?" Diane asked. "Please tell me this isn't another offer to show me your penis, Tom."

Across the fire, John chuckled and I shot him a look. If he let his bride in on the joke, my whole plan would be ruined. Hailey's fingers paused and I squeezed her hand. She knew all about snipe hunting, but loved a practical joke almost as much as I did. I knew

129

she'd play along. As much as we both liked Diane, she needed to be fully initiated into being an islander.

"One time. That was one time. And it was kind of an island tradition." I defended my only serious attempt at hitting on Diane.

Both women snorted and rolled their eyes at my old pick-up line.

"Settle down. First, I have a girlfriend now." I let my eyes meet Hailey's and, as happened a lot when I looked at her, I smiled. I couldn't help it. I was a man in love. "Second, I'm not showing Diane what she's missing. No matter how much you beg. I don't want to break up a marriage." I grinned and gave her both dimples. Our relationship bordered on brother-sister, especially the teasing part.

"Okay, so if it's not another penis euphemism, what is it?" Diane asked again.

"It's a bird," Hailey spoke up. "Very rare, but they're all over the San Juan Islands."

John leaned forward. "Especially around here. Something about the lakes they like."

Diane glanced around the dark woods and lake. "I haven't noticed any unusual birds since we've been here."

"That's because they only come out at night." I set down my beer and rested my elbows on my knees. "You may have heard them. Their birdcall sounds like their name."

"Snipe, snipe," John and Hailey said at the same time. John spoke in a falsetto. I couldn't look at him and keep a straight face.

"Snipe, snipe?" Diane imitated them. "Sounds a little bit like that Monty Python sketch, "The Knights Who Say Ni.""

John met my eyes and raised his eyebrow in a silent challenge. Was she onto us already?

"Not quite the same thing. I don't think they even have snipes in England." I attempted to sound convincing. "They're really cool. Similar to pheasants, but prettier. The males have blue and green feathers, like peacocks. Only smaller. Like the length of my forearm from beak to tail. Their eyes are bright yellow and glow in the dark. That's how you spot them," I babbled.

Diane wrinkled her forehead. "So a nocturnal, pheasant-peacock hybrid with glowing yellow eyes?"

Hailey nodded. "Exactly. They're really cool. It's kind of a rite of passage to see one. Some people try to catch them because…" she paused and stared at the dark lake, "…their feathers are supposed to bring good luck."

Nice recovery.

"Do people eat them?" Diane asked.

"No!" we all said in unison.

"They're protected, like eagles," John said.

"So? This is a thing I need to see while we're here?" Doubt crept into Diane's voice.

"Since it's your first camping trip on San Juan, it's a must!" Hailey sounded overly excited, probably to counteract Diane's growing suspicion. She even bounced in her camp chair, giggling and almost tipping over. That might've been going too far.

I reached out and steadied her chair. No need to go crazy. I suspected she and Diane were both a little more than tipsy.

"What do we need to do? Walk into the woods with flash-lights?" Diane looked at John.

With a straight face, he answered, "It's not that easy. They're shy. You need to be completely quiet. Silent. No laughing." He gave them a stern look.

Both women giggled.

Hailey frowned and pressed her finger to her lips. "Shhh, we're hunting snipes. Be serious."

"Yes, sir." Diane saluted him and giggled louder.

Ignoring them, John continued. "We'd need to gather supplies first. Probably better to break into two groups. One group can set the trap and the other can flush out the birds towards it."

"You guys are good at being loud and causing a ruckus, so I say

Diane and I will sit with the bags and let you two act like bird dogs," Hailey smiled at me.

I love that she was up for scaring her friend. If the prank went well, maybe I'd get a bonus blow job.

"We need bags and flashlights." I set down my beer and stood. "John, don't you have some in the truck?" I jerked my head toward the road.

"Right," he stretched out the word and patted his thighs. "Bags and flashlights coming right up. Guess we're going snipe hunting."

Away from the glow of the fire, the night closed around us. Diane and Hailey's voices, along with quiet laughter, carried through the trees.

"So what's the real plan?" John asked as we walked to his truck.

"Same thing as always: scare the girl."

He clicked the lock and his lights blinked bright orange in the darkness. "You know, they're both a sure thing, right? Pissing them off might not be the best idea." He held up his left hand where the gold from his ring reflected the light.

"I know, but that doesn't mean we can't have some fun. I figure we'll let them wander off, make some noise, then circle back and scare them. We'll all have a good laugh and the adrenaline could make things interesting later."

"It's all about sex with you."

I nodded. No denying my love of sex.

He shook his head and pulled two canvas wood carriers from the back of his cab. "These will have to do. I should have a flashlight in the glove box and there's another one in the cabin."

I clapped my hands and rubbed my palms together. "Excellent."

"You realize Hailey knows all about snipe hunting from when we were kids, right?"

"Yeah, but she loves a good prank as much as we do. At least she likes being on the pranker side."

"I'm still not sure what's in it for me, but if I get in trouble, you're in the dog house with me." He stared me down. He could be intimidating with his giant height and dark beard, but after over twenty years of friendship, I knew he was all glower and no fight.

"Deal."

When we returned to the fire, the girls were whispering with their heads together. John cleared his throat behind me, and both women jumped apart.

"Gossiping?" I asked, trailing my hand over Hailey's shoulder before leaning down to kiss her behind her ear.

She exhaled a shaky breath. "Us? No, never." She reached her hand behind the chair and grazed my upper thigh.

I stepped away before she found her target.

When she tilted her head back to look at me, her mischievous grin told me she knew the exact affect she had on me and my body. She owned me, and we both knew it.

Unable to resist her, I leaned over and gently brushed my lips against hers in an upside down kiss. Her hands wove into my shaggy hair and tugged.

"Ahem. Are you two going to make out or are we going to find these silly birds?" Diane had left her chair and wrapped herself around John. She only came up to his shoulder.

Hailey leaned forward. "I think we should have a bet."

As she stretched and stood to her full height, I eyed her long legs in tight jeans. "Bet?"

She knew there was no such thing as a snipe, what exactly were the stakes?

"Yes, a bet. Whoever finds the first snipe wins."

"What if we can't find any? I don't want to be tromping through these woods all night out there with all sorts of rabid animals. The last thing I need is to be mauled by a crazed woodchuck." Diane's brow furrowed with worry.

I laughed. "I think we could take a woodchuck, if they even lived on the island."

Diane shook her head. "Don't joke. They can be vicious. Especially if they're hungry. Or rabid. I overheard a guy at the lodge mention a cougar sighting."

"Are you sure he was talking about the cat and not the woman?" John asked.

"He was serious. They're nocturnal, too." Diane's eyes widened with fear. A branch snapped in the woods and her head spun around like *The Exorcist*. "What was that?"

"I'll protect you from any fearsome woodland creatures in the dark. The scariest thing will be Tom, I promise." John kissed the top of her head and she looked up at him like he'd hung the stars just for her. The man was tall enough he could probably reach them.

I'd never heard of cougars around here except for in the bars at Friday Harbor. "Ha ha. Okay, let's bet. Snipes you win, cougar you lose?"

"I don't want to jinx ourselves." Worried, Diane looked over her shoulder.

"I bet the two of you can't be quiet," John suggested. "No laughing, giggling or talking. No sounds other than whistles or snipe calls."

"We'll take that bet." Hailey grinned.

John and I laughed.

Both women frowned and crossed their arms over their chests.

"What?" I asked innocently.

"Why do I get a distinct feeling you think we'll lose?" Diane asked.

"Oh no reason." I looked at John for back-up. Once a wingman, always a wingman.

"Well, for one thing, Tom and I are experienced snipe hunters. We're guys. We can go for hours without talking. Plus, I can't think of the last time I giggled," John said smugly.

The women had a silent conversation that ended with both of them rolling their eyes.

"Now, what are we betting for?" I asked.

"We want a day at the spa. The lodge doesn't have one, but Roche Harbor does," Diane declared.

John made eye contact and shrugged. We knew we'd win, so why not agree? "Sure," I said. "Get the works."

Hailey smiled. "And what do you two want?"

Would it be rude to ask for blowjobs? I mean, that would be the obvious answer.

"Hmm…" John stroked his beard.

I tried to telepathically tell him to please say blowjob. It would be better coming from him.

"I'm pretty confident Tom and I can find a snipe or two tonight. I don't want to make you ladies suffer in defeat, so if, I mean, when, we win, I think a grilled steak dinner with baked potatoes and corn, all cooked by our beautiful, sweet women would be a great prize. Don't you think, Donnely?"

Steak?

What happened to blowjobs?

Wait… when was that made-up holiday that combined both? March? Today was August seventh. I mentally counted the months in my head and told myself to mark it on next year's calendar.

"Tom?" Hailey asked.

"What?"

"Steak dinner good for you?"

I frowned and stuck out my bottom lip in a pout. "Sure. Steak's good."

"Since when don't you like steak?" Hailey tugged on my sleeve.

I gazed down into her beautiful green eyes. "Nothing. I love steak."

"Did you want the prize to be something else?" Her fingers grazed mine before she wove them together.

I leaned closer and told her the truth. "I was hoping he'd say blowjobs."

She swatted my arm and laughed. "You know you don't have to earn those," she whispered. "What are you doing later?"

"Let's go find these damn snipes!" I shouted.

The others startled at my booming voice.

"All right. Let's do this." John pointed to the woods behind the cabin. "We'll find a clearing to set the trap, then leave you so we can flush out the snipes."

He stomped off through the trees, his flashlight lighting a narrow path. I followed behind, marking our path so we could find our way back to the lake.

About ten minutes later, we arrived at a small clearing around a large rock and a downed tree. It would be easy to cut through the trees and hide behind the log or sneak up behind the boulder. It was perfect.

"This looks like the perfect spot. If you sit with your backs against the rock, we can funnel the snipes through the ferns, straight into the bags." John spoke with the confidence of an experienced snipe hunter.

"Leave us one of the flashlights," Hailey suggested. "So we can make sure whatever comes through the ferns isn't a raccoon. Or a serial killer."

"Tom, you did leave your hockey mask at home, right?" Diane asked.

I smirked. "I don't usually travel with it. If you see someone wearing one, you better scream and run."

"And lose the bet? No way. I really want a massage." Hailey grinned at me.

My competitiveness flared. The sooner one of them lost, the sooner I could get her alone. I ducked my head to steal a quick kiss.

"May the best team find the snipe," I whispered against her lips and pinched her ass.

She yelped and stepped away. "It's on, Donnely. Bring it."

The girls opened their bags and leaned against the boulder, with their crossed arms and serious game faces. I suddenly felt unwanted.

"Don't forget the snipe call," John called over his shoulder as we retraced our steps down the path.

Diane chirped, "snipe."

We both struggled to contain our laughter.

When we returned to the fire, John pulled out a beer and opened it, offering it to me before he got one for himself. "How long should we let them go on with that?"

I took a long pull from the bottle. "I say at least ten minutes. Let them start listening for rabid forest creatures. A few snapped twigs and rustling leaves will only build up their nerves."

We sat in silence, drinking our beers, and listening to the faint sound of snipe calls and whistles from the woods.

"Ready?" John asked after finishing his beer.

"I am, but I have an idea."

"Why am I afraid to ask about this brilliant idea?" He shook his head.

"I like that you think it's brilliant and you haven't even heard it yet." I jumped out of my chair and unbuttoned my jeans.

CHAPTER 3

"What the hell?" John shouted and moved to the other side of the fire. "Why are you taking off your pants?"

"It's part of my plan." I yanked my jeans over my left boot, lose my balance, and sit on the ground with a thump. "Okay, boots off before jeans would have been smarter."

"Your plan involves being pantsless?"

"I was thinking it would be funnier if we were naked. We could run through the woods. Like streaking."

John's mouth dropped open and he shook his head. "And the point of that is?"

"Dude, other than running naked through the woods?"

"What's up with you being naked outside? Haven't you outgrown this already?"

"Come on. Who doesn't like being naked outside? Next you're going to tell me you don't like to piss outdoors either."

"Every man likes peeing outside. It's one of the joys of being a man."

"Just checking you're still a man. Come on." I unbuttoned my shirt and pulled it and my T-shirt over my head. I stood there in my boxers and boots, goosebumps appearing on my skin. "Hurry up. It's colder than I thought."

"You're insane."

"You're boring."

I stared down my best friend. Back when we were kids, I could talk him into any sort of cockamamie idea I had. Didn't matter that it usually ended with both of us in trouble. Or if I couldn't convince him to join me, I knew he'd bail me out when I screwed up. Now that he was married, our days of being stupid guys felt numbered. Soon he'd probably become a dad, and get all responsible and serious.

Hell, I'd probably be a dad someday, too. Hailey and I hadn't talked about it, but she loved my big family. And I loved her. Someday we'd get married. With the way we had sex all the time, her getting knocked up would be inevitable.

Married with kids.

I shook my head at the thought, but smiled.

"You ready?" John stood there in his boxers and boots.

I gave him a mental high five. "Ready."

I dropped my boxers and ran off into the woods, praying there wasn't poison ivy or stinging nettles around here.

Realizing I was making too much noise, I slowed to a walk. I heard John catch up to me, but I didn't look back. We whistled and called out "snipe" in falsettos to let the girls know we were coming, then cut across the path to the other side. Once we had them thinking we were heading back from the lake, we approached from the opposite direction.

About ten yards ahead, the glow of a flashlight lit the clearing. I held up my hand to let John know to stop. He whistled to catch my attention and then pointed behind the rock. We focused on treading softly through the underbrush in that direction, lest we give ourselves away. John let out a low growl. I covered my mouth to stifle a laugh.

Turned out we didn't need to be so quiet. When we arrived, the clearing was empty.

Except for something wiggling around in one of the canvas bags.

I snuck closer to get a better look. The flashlight lay on the boulder in front of us. There was no sign of the girls.

John whistled and called out "snipe".

We listened for a response. Nothing.

Our eyes met and I jerked my head toward the clearing and the bags. Not wanting to speak, I gestured we should check the perimeter.

Something heavy fell in the woods on the other side of the nurse log, making a thumping sound as it hit the mossy forest floor. Maybe Diane was right about the cougars.

I took a step into the clearing, John right behind me. The bag flipped over. I stopped short, and he bumped into me. We jumped apart and instinctively cupped our junk. No man on man naked touching. Not in the plan.

A flash of movement caught my eye. I spun around and saw silver fur coming straight for me as a raccoon sped between us into the woods.

"Holy fuck," I whispered harshly. Surprised, I stumbled and knocked into John with my naked ass again.

"Dude, what the hell was that?" he all but shouted.

Another raccoon bolted for the woods behind the fallen log. A scream broke the silence of the woods.

I met John's eyes. "Oh, shit."

He moved toward the sound.

A second later, a startled, disheveled Hailey and Diane burst into the clearing from the same direction.

Everyone starting shouting at the same time.

CHAPTER 4

"Did you see that?"

"Did you see the raccoon?"

"Holy shit."

"Why are you naked?"

"I can't believe there were two of them."

"Why weren't you with the bags?"

"Where are your pants?"

"What were you doing in the woods?"

"Are you okay?"

"Snipe!" Diane burst out laughing.

Diane's laughing grew contagious and the rest of us joined her.

"Did you really think I didn't know about snipe hunting?" She wheezed, breathless and bent over with her hands on her thighs.

Hailey stood in front of me. I couldn't tell if she was shielding me from Diane or facing me to avoid looking at John in his underwear. "Seriously, why are you naked?"

"And why aren't you?" Diane tugged on the hem of John's boxers, clearly flirting with him.

"I only get naked with you." He kissed her forehead.

Hailey giggled. "You didn't answer my question, Tom."

"It's the woods." I shrugged. My explanation was completely logical. "I thought it would be funnier to be naked."

"What is it with you being naked outside?" she asked, not expecting an answer.

"Is this an ongoing thing?" Diane sounded curious.

"Oh, like you don't have an outdoor shower." I pointed at her.

Diane at least pretended to look embarrassed.

A beam of light swept across our group.

"Care to explain what you folks are doing out here? I could hear yelling from down the road."

"Uh oh," I mumbled under my breath.

A ranger stood at the edge of the clearing.

"Good evening, sir." John simultaneously greeted our new friend and pulled Diane in front of himself. "We're snipe hunting."

Guess we were going with the truth. I managed to keep my expression serious. Hailey turned around to face the ranger, but pressed her back to my chest.

"Snipes, you say?" The ranger flashed his light across our faces. "Never heard of naked snipe hunting. This is a family place, you know. We don't tolerate any sort of public nudity or other indecent activities."

I snorted and tried to cover it with a cough. "No, sir. We, um…" I tried to think of a reason two grown men, one naked and one in only his boxers, would be in the woods in the middle of the night. "…Well…"

"They lost a bet," Diane spoke up. "If we didn't find a snipe, they had to strip."

Ranger Bob scanned the area. "Don't see any clothes. Or snipes."

"Our clothes are back by the fire pit," I explained. "It's kind of a long story."

"I figured as much. Pretty sure we don't have any snipes around here, but you all knew that, didn't you?"

I couldn't tell if he was pissed off or amused. Or both.

We all nodded.

"We do have a raccoon problem down at this end of the cabins. You wouldn't want to encounter one of those while you're out here sharing what the Lord gave you with the rest of nature." He stared at me.

John's laugh rang out. "Too late for that. All that hollering and noise you heard was us encountering a pair of raccoons."

The ranger's light fell on an empty bag of corn nuts lying on the ground. "Not too smart to leave food or garbage around. You're asking for trouble." From his deep frown, he didn't see the humor in our prank. "Let that be a lesson to you. Now head on back to your cabin and we'll forget the entire incident. I know I'm going to pretend I didn't see anything."

John picked up the bags while we promised to not leave food or trash out before saying goodnight to the ranger. He looked like he was fighting to keep his face serious and respectful.

"Last one to the fire is raccoon bait," I yelled and took off in a sprint back to the fire and the dignity of my clothes. I had my boxers and T-shirt on by the time the others tromped out of the woods. The fire had died down during our hunt, so I prodded it back to life and resumed my spot in the camp chair.

Hailey pulled her chair close to mine and kissed my cheek.

"What was that for?"

"Giving me yet another naked Tom story for when I need a good laugh."

I cupped her cheek and kissed her.

"Speaking of naked, want to go skinny dipping?" I doubted I could convince her to do it knowing our friendly local ranger could interrupt us at any time. What a waste.

"No way! Not with a ranger and crazy raccoons lurking in the woods. My luck there would be a lake monster, too. Or Jason." She grinned at me.

I rubbed my cheekbone in memory of last Halloween. "No more hockey masks. I promise."

"Speaking of things that go bump in the woods, we heard something fall right before the raccoon and all hell broke out. Was that one of you?" John asked.

Diane and Hailey started giggling.

"We were hiding and planning to scare you. Hailey tripped and fell into me, then I tumbled over too. I'm surprised you couldn't hear us trying to stifle our laughter. We were rolling around on our backs like a pair of turtles."

"Sexy," I commented. Not that I had fantasies of the two of them naked. Nope. Not my best friend's wife.

"At least we weren't naked, you big dorks."

"A dork is a whale penis," Diane said with a straight face.

We all turned to look at her.

"What? It is! You can look it up online. Or you could if we had cell service."

"Then I guess it's an accurate name for me." I gave her a cocky smile.

"Don't be too smug, Tom. Remember I saw you naked not even thirty minutes ago." Diane laughed and sat on John's lap. "Don't take this the wrong way, dear husband, but you're an even bigger dork than Tom."

John wrapped his arms around his wife and shot me a grin over her shoulder.

"Before Thor starts pouting, I think we're going to call it a night." Hailey chuckled, pulling herself out of her chair, and holding out her hand to me.

When we were both standing, she leaned close and whispered in my ear. "I believe you said something earlier about a blowjob."

She didn't need to mention it again. I practically dragged her back to the cabin. When she didn't move fast enough, I picked her up and threw her over my shoulder.

From her upside down position, she called out goodnight to John and Diane.

"Spa day tomorrow," Diane said back.

"Don't you mean steak dinner?" John asked.

"Let's call it a tie and everyone wins," I said as I set Hailey down by the cabin's door.

"I love it when everyone wins. Especially when it's a tie," she whispered.

Her words conjured up all sorts of possibilities. Possibilities involving her naked were much better than being naked in the woods with a raccoon.

"This is the life. I could live like this all the time." I stretched my arms and patted my stomach. "Hot women cooking me steak while I sit around like a king."

"I hear you. A man could get used to this." John pushed his empty plate away.

"How is this different than most of the rest of your lives? We're still on an island, only it's a different one than home." Hailey sipped her wine. She had a sleepy, content expression on her face and if she leaned any further back in her chair, she'd be horizontal.

"True, but there's no work here. We get up, fish, get fed, laze around. It's pretty much heaven." John poured more wine for Hailey.

"I have to admit this kind of camping isn't too bad." Diane's skin glowed. So did Hailey's. They'd come back from the spa smelling of flowers, and all soft. I couldn't wait to get Hailey naked.

"Let's make it a semi-annual trip," Hailey suggested.

"I agree. And when we have kids, we can still come back in the summers." Diane's lips curved into a small smile

John and I both choked on our beers.

"Kids?" he sputtered. "Not any time soon, though, right?"

Diane's smile grew and his eyes widened as she gently rubbed her stomach.

GIVE AND TAKE

A MODERN LOVE STORY AND WINGMEN
CROSSOVER SHORT

INTRODUCTION

Originally published in the Red Hot Holidays anthology, this short is crammed with as many characters from Modern Love Stories and Wingmen as I could manage. I like to imagine it's a holiday special of my favorite TV series where everyone comes home for the holidays. Written in multiple POVs, I thought it would be fun to hear from Diane and Hailey as well as the guys.

***

It's Christmastime on Whidbey.
Join the holiday fun with the characters from Daisy's Wingmen and Modern Love Stories series.
You never know who will show up at the annual Sip 'n Stroll in Langley.
Someone's pregnant.
Someone's engaged.
And someone gets a puppy.

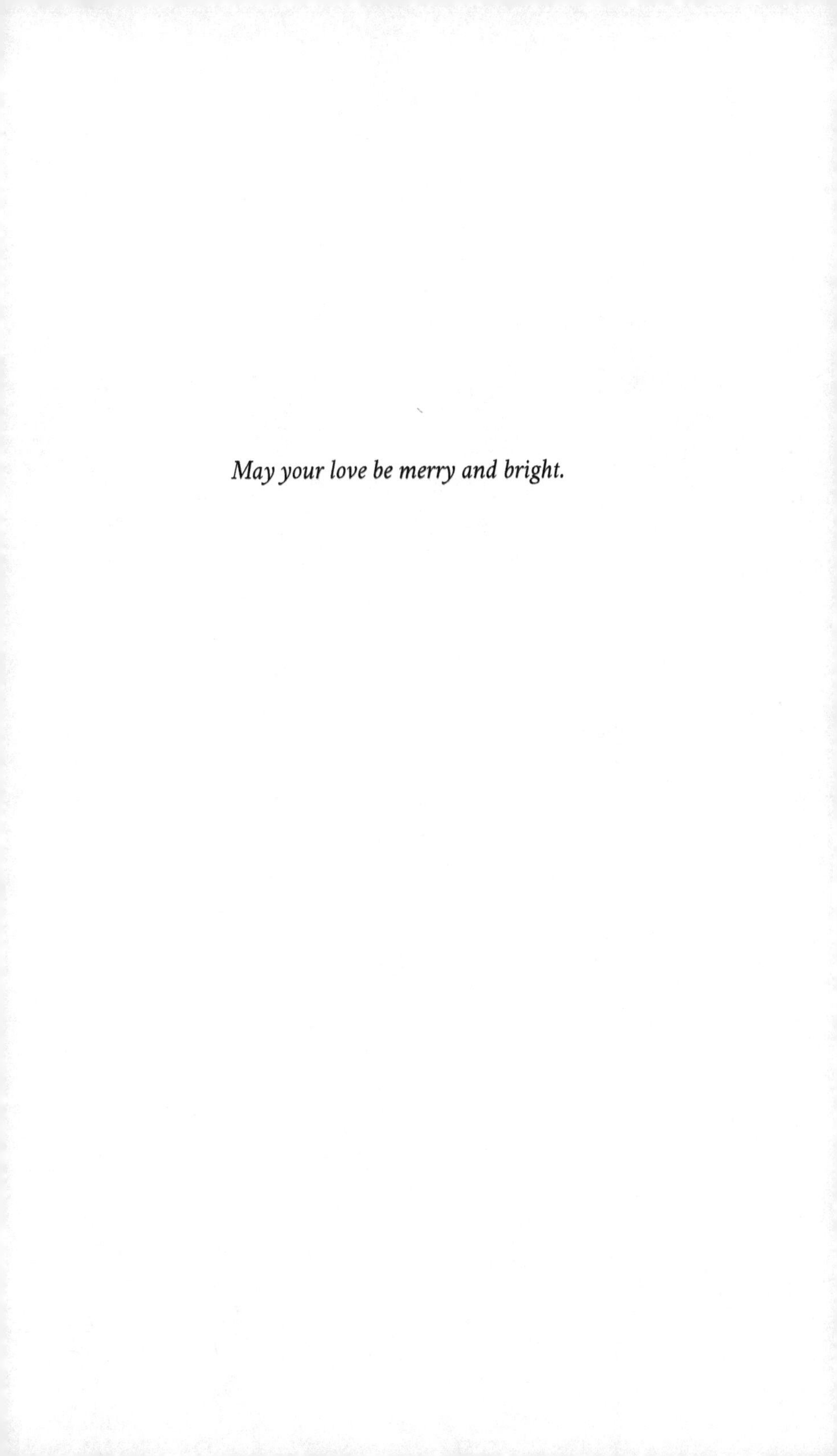

May your love be merry and bright.

CHAPTER 1

JOHN

Hailey opens the small crate hidden under a blanket in the cargo area of her SUV. "He's a Labradoodle."

A tiny brown dustball of a puppy stumbles out and blinks at us. I pick him up and cradle him in the crook of my arm. The pup snuggles into my flannel shirt and softly nibbles the cloth. "Are you sure? He looks kind of small for eight weeks."

"I'm sure. The breeder said he'll get big, bigger than a normal Lab."

I examined the puppy's tiny paws. "Not sure about that. Aren't you supposed to be able to tell by the size of the feet?"

"I thought that was for penises, not dogs." She blurts out and blushes.

"I think it works for both." I need to change the subject. No way am I talking about penis size with Hailey.

As if he knows we're talking about him, the brown fluff ball barks. The sound is a squeaky yip.

"What are you going to name him?" I let him bite on my shirt with his sharp teeth. Those things are like tiny razors.

"I figured Tom could name him, but I'm partial to Gus."

"Just don't let him name the dog after his boat. One Master Baiter is enough." I scratch the top of the dog's head.

"Knowing him he'll pick something like Carhartt or Stihl. He's pretty predictable." She tugs her knit cap down over her short hair against the chilly breeze off the bay. December at the beach is quiet and beautiful, but also cold and damp. Most of the houses are empty this time of year.

"How long do we get him for?" I pull my shirt free from the puppy's mouth. He nips at my finger, but doesn't draw blood. Maybe they should name him Sharky.

"I want to surprise him after the Sip 'n Stroll. I don't think I can wait any longer than that."

This weekend is the annual holiday event in Langley. It's a draw for locals and tourists alike. Back in our wingmen days, Tom dubbed it the Sip 'n Troll when we'd set up at the Dog House tavern to share holiday cheer. Those days are, thankfully, long over. I think I can speak for both of us when I say our lives are better off now. Way better. Whole different world.

Nodding, I say, "I can keep him here until the weekend. I'll put his crate upstairs in the spare room so Babe doesn't bother him." My Lab might not approve of a new dog in the house. Poor guy doesn't realize just how much his world is going to change in a few months.

"Thanks, John. I know how much Tom hates surprises, but he's been hinting about a dog for months. It was either this or another fish."

"The one he got at the fair last summer didn't last a weekend. Are you sure he can handle a mammal?" Poor fish was half-dead before we even finished the lumberjack competition. Tom was ridiculously proud that he won it for Hailey, he bragged to all the kids surrounding him at the duck pond game. Never mind it was a kids' game to begin with. The man wanted a fish, he won a fish.

"Poor Orca." Hailey frowns and pulls down the sleeves of her sweater, tucking her hands into the thick wool. "Now that we're living together, I'll be in charge of keeping nameless here alive."

The puppy lifts his head at her voice and squirms in my arms. "They're both lucky to have you."

Hailey and I don't spend much time together without Diane or Tom around, but I like her. The two women have become close friends, and whatever she does to manage Tom seems to be working. He's never been happier.

"Likewise. Honestly, I can't believe I'm living with Tom Donnely."

"A year ago if you told me, I never would've believed it. Maybe if he was renting out a room." I scratch my beard and give her a smile. "He's not making you pay rent is he?" Tom inherited his land and built the house himself. He doesn't have a mortgage and other than property taxes has no expenses other than utilities. But he can be cheap too.

"I tried to pay him once for a tank of propane. That didn't end well." She rolls her eyes at my best friend's stubborn nature. "He's oddly traditional when it comes to being a man and providing for his woman."

"That doesn't surprise me. He takes after Pops more than he'll admit."

"We all miss his grand-dad. Sometimes I like to think Clifford's ghost gave Tom the kick in the ass he needed. Is that terrible of me?"

"If anyone could come back and haunt us, it would be Clifford Donnely." I hand the puppy back to her. She nuzzles his head with her nose before putting him into the crate. Nameless burrows into the blanket and closes his eyes.

"How's Diane feeling these days? I haven't spoken to her since last week."

"She's good. Eating, sleeping more. Otherwise the same." I don't mention we've entered the crazy horny stage of her pregnancy. Now that she's not throwing up anymore, all she wants to do is eat and have sex. If it weren't for her giant boobs, I'd say she was turning into a super horny teenage boy.

"Look at you, John Day, married man and dad to be." She grins at me. I've known Hailey most of my life, and despite the events of the past year, it's tough not to see her as little Lori Donnely's tough-as-nails tomboy friend.

"I could say the same thing about you, Hailey. Well, not the married or pregnant part …" I let the last part trail off. I don't really want to discuss my best friend's sex life with his girlfriend. Ever.

She slowly blinks her eyes and shakes her head. "No on both the last two. We're not really going to talk about sex, are we? Please say no."

"God, no." I take a step back. "Nope. Don't ask, don't tell."

She closes the crate door and picks it up by the handle. "On that note, I'm going to head home." She hands me the crate and a bag of puppy food. "I was never here. We never had this conversation."

I nod and settle the bag under my arm, holding the crate with the other hand. "What conversation?"

With a wave she walks to the front of her car.

It's a good thing she's leaving. Our conversations should never involve penis size or sex lives. Plus, I'd gotten too close to blowing Tom's plans for the weekend by bringing up marriage.

***

Christmas has exploded all over Langley. As I pull into a parking spot on Second Street, I note that every storefront is covered with holiday greenery and festive decorations. Some windows are painted with winter scenes, including a pod of Orcas wearing Santa hats at the music store, while others have enough mistletoe draped everywhere to poison the entire town.

The holiday stroll doesn't officially start for another hour, but

I told Diane I'd meet her early. Christmas carols play through the speakers hidden under the buildings' eaves as I make my way down the path to her Pilates studio. She bought the business from Traci this fall. Once the baby comes, she'll need someone else to take over her classes for a while, but having her own business makes her happy, and I love anything that makes her happy.

I pause outside the building and think about how casually I just thought about the baby. My baby. Our baby. After the shock wore off, I've slowly adjusted to the thought that in a few months, I'm going to be a dad. Me. With a kid. Hell, we have years before he'll be a full blown kid. Baby.

By the way, baby is a four letter word. I've said a lot of four letter words over the years, but baby has become my new favorite.

Smiling at what a huge softie this whole pregnancy has made me, I shake my head and open the door to the studio. Diane sits on a mat on the floor, stretching. Her belly protrudes enough she can no longer reach her toes. With her dark hair pulled back, the mirror reflects her cleavage as she leans forward. It's my favorite part of her ever-changing body.

She catches me staring and sits up, grinning. I swear she leans back on her hands in order to push out her chest, and tease me further. "You are so predictable, husband of mine."

I walk over and stand in front of her. The view is even better from this angle. Her workout tank cuts low, giving me a spectacular eye-full.

"Are you going to stand there ogling my boobs, or will you help my fat ass off the floor?" Her cheeks are pink from exercise. Or the tightness in my jeans. She is almost eye level with my fly and I'm certain she can see how she affects me.

Still. Every day.

Always.

I extend both my hands and lift her up. Fat ass? Never.

I pull her to me and remind her how beautiful she is. My hand cups her head as the other supports her back, dipping her slightly as my lips find hers, I moan a little when she weaves her fingers into my hair and tugs. Her strong grip on my bicep tells me she is as turned on as I am right now. If it weren't for the fact the glass doors are unlocked and all the lights are on, I'd take this much further right now. Forget the holiday stroll. *Why didn't I lock the door when I came in?*

Her stomach rumbles. Loudly. It sounds like a motorcycle revving. Or a bear growling.

I break the kiss because I'm laughing.

She tightens her hand on my arm and pulls me back down with her fingers in my hair. Her moan is of frustration. "Ignore the monster demanding food. Kiss me."

I peck her lips. It's all I can do because now I'm smiling and chuckling, and there is no way I can kiss her properly.

Her lips pout, full of disappointment. "You're laughing at a poor pregnant woman."

"I'm laughing that your stomach sounds like a bear. It's my husbandly duty to feed you and worry about your ankles swelling." I glance down to make sure her ankles aren't swollen. From this angle, I can't even see her ankles because of her belly.

"They're fine. I'm fine."

Her stomach grumbles again. This time it's a low rumble. The mountain is angry. I pat her bump. "We'll stop and get you a snickerdoodle at the bakery."

"Mmm … I do love those." She stretches up on her toes to give me a soft kiss. "You're the most wonderful husband ever."

I run my hands down her side and over her hips, which have also become more curvier in the last couple months. "I do what I can."

"Let me change and I'll be ready to go. What time are we meeting Tom and Hailey?" She steps away and heads toward the changing room.

I glance at the clock on the wall. "We've got about fifteen minutes before we said we'd meet them.

She stops walking and gives me a slow smile. Her tongue runs along the edge of her top teeth.

I can't believe I'm turning this down. "We don't have time."

"We have plenty of time."

I close my eyes to this temptress and exhale. On a normal evening, we'd have plenty of time for something fun, but not tonight. Not for the surprise I've arranged. There isn't enough time for Diane to shower and get ready. We can't show up smelling of sex. Not tonight.

"Are you turning down some hanky-panky?" Her mouth drops open in disbelief.

Staring at her inviting lips reminds me of the wood I'm half sporting since the kiss a few minutes ago. We wouldn't have to have full out sex …

I've about convinced myself to offer a compromise, when cold air hits my back from the opening of the front door.

Should've locked it.

"There you are," Hailey exclaims as she walks into the space. A knit hat covers her hair and a puffy coat makes her look like she's wearing a sleeping bag. After unwrapping her long knit scarf, she stops, her focus bouncing between us. "Oh. Am I interrupting something?"

Beard burn has deepened the pink on Diane's cheeks. Her hair is mostly out of its ponytail. She looks thoroughly kissed. Blushing deeper, she dashes into the small changing room and shuts the door. "Be right out!"

Hailey stares at me.

I rub my hand over my beard again.

"I was totally interrupting something! I'm so sorry." She focuses on the window instead of meeting my eyes. "It's cold and I'm early, so I thought I'd grab Diane and then meet up with Tom, but you're here already, and Diane's not changed yet, so she's not ready, but you're wearing your jacket and I'm not sure even what's going on, but the look you two were giving each other could melt metal, and now I'm babbling. So this is awkward."

I don't know if she breathed at all while she said all that. Pretty sure she didn't.

"It's fine. You didn't interrupt."

She meets my eyes. "I don't believe you, but okay."

We stand there awkwardly for a minute.

I brush a hand over my beard. "I dropped off the puppy at your house on my way over here. I also let him out, so he should be fine for a couple of hours."

"Thanks for taking him. I owe you."

Luckily, Diane's a fast changer. She exits the room wearing those black leggings she lives in these days and a big sweater.

Hailey makes a cooing sound like a dove when she sees her. "You got bigger this week. I think you popped."

Is popping a good thing?

Diane doesn't appear so sure. "Suddenly, I'm huge." She rubs her belly and smiles down at her hand. Some weird pride or other emotion lodges itself in my throat at seeing her loving expression.

Huge softie. But I'll deny it if anyone asks or comments.

"Where's Tom?" I need reinforcement. I need my wingman. I stare out the glass doors. All I can see is a reflection of the three of us. It's only five o'clock, but it's completely dark out already.

"He's running late, but said he'll find us." Hailey smiles at Diane, reaching out to touch her belly. "Can I feel?"

"Sure. Sometimes the baby kicks after I've been stretching. I don't think she likes it."

Hailey's eyes widen. "She?"

Diane nods. "Well, this week I think she's a she. John's being old fashioned and doesn't want to know the sex until the birth."

"I'm convinced he's a boy." I cross my arms. Boys I can handle. Little girl? I'm not ready for that. I know too much about guys like Tom and me to be able to survive raising a girl.

The two women give me sympathetic frowns, but amusement flashes in their eyes.

"What?"

Diane flattens her expression. "Nothing, honey. Girl or boy, you're going to be an amazing poppa."

My neck prickles in embarrassment. This is too much.

"I'm going to stop by and check on Olaf at the Dog House before this thing starts. You know how he gets cranky when there's going to be a big crowd and a whole hullabaloo."

"Right, Olaf gets cranky." Diane nods. "Sweet of you to check on him. We'll catch up with you in a bit."

"Okay." I rub my neck. "Good. I'll text Tom and tell him to meet me there."

I give her a quick peck on the cheek and nod good-bye to Hailey.

Their heads are together in whispered conversation before the door closes behind me.

I need a beer and some testosterone.

I text Tom.

He replies in a few seconds that he'll meet me at the Dog.

I laugh at my best friend. He knows me well.

CHAPTER 2

TOM

"Hey, Tom." Erik Kelso is setting up a bar stool outside the front door of the Dog House as I cross the street. His Santa hat droops over the left side of his head. He resembles an oversized elf.

"Pretty cold out here for sidewalk drinking." I stop next to his perch. The forecast is for flurries and the damp night air is cold enough for snow. "Or is Olaf carding tonight?"

"Ha, when was the last time Olaf paid for a bouncer?" Pointing above our heads, he gives me a grin. Hanging over us is a ball of mistletoe. I step back and away from its shadow. All along the street, balls of greenery and mistletoe decorate the doorways. Some shops even have chalkboards outside to tally kisses. I have to give the guy credit for the stool.

"Nice," I tell him.

He holds up his fist for a bump. "I figure why try to work the entire street, when I can sit here comfortably and wait for the ladies to come to me. Carter is pissed he didn't think of it first."

I look around for the other Kelso brother, but don't see him inside at the bar.

"Carter's down the block at the pizzeria. We decided to divide and conquer."

Resembling big yellow puppies, the two of them could be John and I a few years ago. I hate to admit it, but their game might even be better than ours. I never thought to set up a stool under a kissing ball. That's horny guy genius at work right there.

"The women won't know what to do with themselves." I bump his fist, giving him his deserved props.

"Speaking of women, does Hailey have any clue what you're planning for Christmas?"

I shake my head. "So far, nope. You guys coming over tomorrow to help me? The girls are scheduled to head over to Seattle to go shopping for the day. I figure we can get the framing up while they're gone. It's all loaded on the flatbed over at the farmhouse."

As weird as it might seem, I'm liking, hell, even enjoying, living with Hailey. Sharing the house and especially my bed with her has been easier than I imagined.

However, sharing a shop space between a welder and a carver has been less than ideal. My barn is big enough for the two of us, but wood and sparks aren't a great mix. So I'm building a small shop for her. That way she can listen to all the Backstreet Boys music she wants.

She'd kill me if I told anyone she still loves '90s boy bands, but I don't think people would be shocked if they found out. The new shop will be pretty small, under a thousand square feet, but vented and all open for her torches. She can still store stuff in the barn.

"What's the plan for tomorrow?" Erik asks.

"We're loading up the framing on the flatbed in the morning. I poured the foundation a couple of weeks ago when she and her mom went on a girls' weekend. It's been covered under a tarp so she doesn't get suspicious."

"She's not suspicious about a tarp in the yard?" He gives me a doubtful look.

"I threw a bunch of carvings and stumps on it and then covered those with another tarp."

He nods in support of my genius. "You're a duplicitous bastard, Donnely. How'd you ever get a hot babe like Hailey?"

"Big word. You studying to pass your GED?"

"Ha ha. I graduated college. I'm just saying you being all monogamous is pretty strange." He lifts his pint glass to take a swig.

Smug asshole. I flick the bottom of the glass, causing it to over tip, spilling a thin stream of beer down the front of his jacket.

He sputters and wipes at the beer. "Hey! What was that for?"

I shoot him a dirty look. "That's for suggesting I'd ever cheat on Hailey."

His eyebrows furrow and his mouth hangs open a little. "I'd never do that. You aren't that stupid. And even if you were, I'd be first in line to console her."

I swat at his head. "There's going to be no need for you, or anybody else, to console Hailey. She's mine and I plan to keep it that way. For a long time. Forever. Got it?"

He holds up his hands. "Got it. Damn, you're so sensitive these days. You and John both are whipped hard."

"You should be so lucky." I laugh and cuff his shoulder before opening the door.

"I'm trying to get lucky. Why do you think I've got my stool here?" His chuckle fades as I enter the bar.

Olaf grumbles hello and puts two pint glasses on the old wood bar. "That kid's going to be trouble tonight."

"You didn't have to serve him. Or give him the stool." I knock on the window to scare Erik. He bounces off the stool and it tumbles over. Flipping me the bird, he straightens up and resumes his seat.

Olaf's laughter turns into a cough. "Eh, he's better out there in the cold than in here where he bothers me. At least I don't have to listen to him."

I sip the foam off of the pint he pours for me. Outside, more people pass by on the sidewalk, their cheerful voices carrying through the glass.

"Damn revelers," Olaf mutters.

"You seem in fine holiday spirits, tonight, O." I spin on my stool to observe him. For as old as he is, and he's got to be in his sixties now, he's still pretty spry. Or maybe ornery is the word I mean.

"Bah humbug." He scowls. "There's going to be caroling later. If people want to sing, that's fine, but standing outside someone's place of business and singing at them feels like harassment. If I wanted to hear all those women singing off-key, I'd go to church. You see me in church on Sunday, Tom?"

I raise my eyebrows. "Can't say that I have, O. Then again, I'd have to be there to see you."

"That's my point exactly."

My gaze flicks left to right as I try to figure out his point. That we're both sinners? "Not following you."

"All this fuss and cheer. I don't need it." He gestures at the strand of multi-colored lights in the window and the faded paper Santas taped to the walls in a couple of places. It's not exactly a holiday wonderland in here.

"Nice kissing ball outside, O," John says as he sits on the stool next to me.

Olaf practically spits. "They hung that up this morning without my permission. Now that Kelso boy has taken up residence underneath it for the night. Probably going to nurse that one beer and scare away my paying customers, too."

John faces me with an alarmed look in his eyes. His beard twitches as he fights a smile. "Olaf seems to be in a good mood."

I nod, struggling not to laugh. "Where are Hailey and Diane?"

"They'll be here in a bit. I left them at the studio, cooing over babies." He takes a long pull on the beer O set in front of him.

We both silently drink our beers and stare out the window past the colorful lights.

John breaks the silence. "You get the ring from your grandmother?"

"Yeah. It's in my glove box." I even locked it just in case. "I had to swear Gramma to secrecy. She wanted to tell my mom. Mom would tell Lori and there wouldn't be any point in trying to surprise Hailey."

"I almost mentioned something at the studio."

"What the hell, dude?" I stare at him. "You what?"

"Calm down. I didn't. Hailey walked in on Diane and me … not full out, but you know, and I got flustered."

"Dude."

"I know, I know. It's serious business. I'm still kind of surprised you're doing it so soon." He takes a swig.

"If Pops taught me anything, it's that life is short. Why wait if I know this is forever?"

John spins his own wedding ring around his finger. "I understand. Completely."

"You're on schedule for Diane's surprise?" I ask.

"Should be. I got a text from Maggie that she was at SeaTac about an hour ago. She and Gil are driving up from Portland for the weekend. Turns out, she's picking up more friends who have a flight around the same time, so they're taking two cars. It's all working out perfectly. "

"That's pretty cool your neighbor was willing to help you out, considering."

He arches his eyebrow. "Considering?"

"What a crush you had on her and how she flirted with you."

"Yeah, that's ancient history. I owe her big time for renting to Diane."

I nod in agreement. Movement outside the window catches my eye. "Speak of the wife …"

Diane waves at us, while Hailey chats up Kelso. With a jolt, I notice *my* girlfriend is standing directly under the kissing ball.

Oh, hell no.

I bolt from my stool, leaving it rattling behind me as I rush the door.

CHAPTER 3

HAILEY

Strong arms wrap around me from behind, pulling me off my feet and spinning me onto the sidewalk. I squeal and thrash about until Tom's voice whispers against my ear.

"If anyone is going to be kissing you tonight, tomorrow, or any other night for the foreseeable future, it's going to be me. Me. No one else." His breath warms my ear and cheek. He sets me down, turning me to face him.

Before I can ask him what the hell is going on, his lips crash onto mine. His mouth is demanding, claiming. I can't breathe, but I don't dare stop kissing him. Not that I have a choice. Oxygen is overrated.

My body responds to him. I press myself closer, wishing I didn't have this puffy jacket creating a down version of bubble-wrap between us. My hands go to his face, anchoring him to me. His arms wrap around my waist.

"Well, that mistletoe seems to be working." An older woman's voice breaks through the sound of my blood pumping in my ears. I break away from Tom's mouth. I can feel the heat from his beard on my cheeks and chin. I look up to see we're standing underneath a ball of mistletoe.

"That was one helluva kiss you two. I'd say get a room, but you're already living together." Erik's sporting a smug smile. I forgot he was sitting here. Diane's studying the greenery above the chocolate shop next door, avoiding our make out session.

Tom's arms are locked around my waist. We're blocking the entire sidewalk and the door to the bar.

"Was it the mistletoe or did you miss me?" I try to pull away, but he tightens his hold.

"I missed you." He gives me a peck on the mouth. "Missed you." He kisses me softly. "So much."

I arch back so I can see him. "And?"

He slowly blinks at me. It's his innocent look. For when he's up to no good or has done something he thinks will piss me off.

With a slow exhale, he releases me, but grabs my hand in his. "Kelso looked like he was going in for the kill with you standing under the mistletoe. I couldn't let that happen." He glowers at Kelso, who gives him a wolfish grin.

Part of me wants to be mad. I don't need a man getting all territorial over me like a dog toy. On the other hand, when Tom gets jealous, he gets this look on his face that I find ridiculously hot. Like he's about to drag me back to his cave. I'll never admit to him that I like it. Or how much it turns me on. Never. He's ego is big enough already.

"Tom ..." I try to pull my hand back.

"Hailey ..." He pulls me closer. I try to resist. I do. I step back and dig in my heels. He's stronger than me and when I give in, I fall into his arms. "I can't help it. I don't trust those Kelsos." He leans down to kiss me, but I sense him eyeing Erik behind me.

A group of a dozen carolers surround us, singing enthusiastically and very loudly, forcing us to move out of their way.

"Here We Come a-wassailing,
among the leaves so green.
Here we come a-wandering,
so fair to be seen.

Love and joy come to you,
and to your wassail, too..."

Diane shelters herself in the doorway of the shop next door. Only the ball on her knit hat is visible. I can barely make out the top of John's dark head in the Dog House's doorway. Erik on his stool, Tom, and I make up a strange audience trio.

Tom backs us up so we have the window behind us. Our legs hit the bench below it and we sit down. Might as well. There's no escaping the horde of singers.

My eyes meet his and we widen them in a silent conversation.

He leans toward me and whispers in my ear, "What's a wassail?"

Without turning my head, and with a forced smile on my face, I whisper back, "I have no idea, but it's both a noun and a verb."

Thankfully, the song comes to an end. Sadly, we never learn the definition of wassail.

We clap and smile, and clap some more. Amongst the brightly dressed revelers, I spot Sally in a Christmas sweater with Rudolph and his red nose blinking on her chest. Next to her is Sandy, in an equally bright holiday sweater, covered in three-dimensional, sparkly tinsel. Both are outdone by Connie's sweater. Her chest is covered with a puffy Christmas tree, complete with ornaments hanging off of it and strings of lights, which are also blinking. Combined, the blinking and sparkling could give someone a seizure. What's a word for beyond tacky?

"Happy Holidays!" they shout at us in over-zealous merriment. I grip Tom's hand. Honestly, I'm a little afraid right now.

Tom flinches beside me.

We wish them the same. John squeezes past Erik to join us.

"Oh, John. We didn't see you there. Where is that lovely wife of yours?" Connie cranes her neck to look around him, as if he's shielding Diane behind him. I wouldn't blame him if he did.

"Oh, look John, you're under the mistletoe." Sally purrs, slinking toward him.

You've never seen a man move so fast. I nearly choke on my laugh.

"Hailey." Erik points above my head.

Damn mistletoe is everywhere. I give Tom a quick peck. He isn't expecting it. I get mostly cheek and beard.

"Where is Diane?" John scans the crowd.

"She's over there." I point to the empty doorway. "Or she was."

A few seconds later, Diane appears with a waffle cone in her gloved hand. It looks to be a triple scoop of chocolate ice cream.

With a sheepish smile, she greets us. "I got hungry waiting for the singing to finish. I wasn't sure how long it was going to last. And John promised me a cookie earlier, so I had sweets on my mind." She licks the cone and closes her eyes in pleasure. Opening them again, she asks, "Anyone want some?"

We all decline.

"We wanted to let you know we started a pool on the baby at the bank," Connie chirps with delight. "People have to guess the date, time and the sex, since you won't tell us."

"We have another one going at the grocery store." Sandy adds. "A dollar a guess. We're up to thirty-five dollars so far, and it's only been up this week."

John grumbles and walks over to Diane. "You're betting on my baby?"

Diane's hand on his arm stops his grumbling. "Oh, that's sweet. Please don't feel hurt, but we're not telling anyone the sex because we don't know it."

"And I think it's actually called gender now." John's voice is calm like he's talking to young children.

The three women murmur and smile at him in return. There's a flurry of oohs and aahs when Diane pats her belly.

It's a little disturbing. I wonder if she feels like a prized heifer these days. I wonder if I'll feel like a cow when I'm pregnant.

If.

I mean I'm not planning to get pregnant right now. I wasn't

like Lori growing up–always counting the number of kids I'd have.

If.

Tom and I haven't even been dating that long. Yes, we're living together. Yes, I love him. But we're not ready for kids. Not like Diane. She was ready the second she and John got married. Maybe even before then.

Although, little Toms running around would be really cute. Floppy blond hair and his dimples in a pint size person? Adorable.

But that's a long way off. Like marriage. We haven't even talked about getting married. I mean I'm not opposed to it, but he's just getting used to having a serious, adult relationship and a girlfriend.

There's no rush.

If, not when. I'm barely thirty. We have plenty of time for us before we start thinking about kids.

Tom squeezes my fingers. I glance up at him. His eyes hold so much love for me. Reflecting the Christmas lights all around us, he's the most handsome man I've ever known. Growing up, he was the cutest boy I'd ever seen. I never believed he could be mine.

Okay, maybe *when* we have kids.

For now we'll have the puppy. That's a good place to start our little family.

The carolers finally move down to the next group of shops, leaving the four of us on the sidewalk. Erik's disappeared, too.

"Shall we stroll?" Diane breaks off a piece of the cone.

John leans over and steals a big bite of her ice cream.

"Hey!" She moves it away from his mouth. "No stealing from the pregnant girl."

"Let's mosey." Tom holds out his arm for me to take. It's an old fashioned romantic gesture. Totally unexpected from him and completely sweet. I tuck my arm with his and he holds my hand.

John and Diane lead the way down First Street. Diane finishes off the ice cream in record time and starts talking about finding mulled cider. We step into the street to avoid the crowd trapped by a boisterous rendition of "Up on the Housetop," complete with noisemakers and sound effects.

"Diane!" A woman with shoulder-length blondish red hair calls out from the other side of the carolers. She's wearing a giant plaid scarf the size of a blanket.

"John!" Now she's walking toward us. A really handsome older guy with salty-gray-brown hair follows her. He has the whole hot professor look going for him in a blazer and jeans.

CHAPTER 4

MAGGIE

"*M*aggie!" Diane rushes over to us, not looking either way when she crosses the street. It's a little worrisome.

I know it's tiny Langley. Most nights you could lie down in the middle of any street and not get run over, but I don't think John could survive if anything happened to her. Especially now that she's pregnant.

I've never seen a man more ridiculously excited about having a baby, but in a stoic, classic John way. He smiles more and laughs more. He's always watching her to make sure she's okay.

Now that John's happily married and starting a family, Gil has warmed up to him. He doesn't even frown when John's name comes up anymore. As if there was ever any real competition there.

Diane hugs me while John says hello to Gil. Clearly, Diane hasn't spotted part of her big surprise behind us yet.

John and I wave at each other. He cocks his head in question and I jerk mine back to answer him.

"What brings you to the island?" he asks innocently. Too innocently. He might as well be whistling in nonchalance.

Diane stares at him, clearly suspecting him of something. She studies me and then goes back to staring at him. "You two are acting odd. What are you up to?"

Beside me, Gil chuckles. I elbow him.

He rocks back on his heels. "I've never been to the Sip 'n Stroll, so I demanded some holiday cheer after turning in my final grades. Maggie agreed and suggested we spend Christmas on the beach this year."

Diane nods, but her eyes still hold doubt.

"You are the worst surprisers in surprise history!"

Diane's eyes widen at the voice shouting behind us.

"Surprise!" Quinn shoves me out of the way. "Look who's here!"

I stumble, but Gil steadies me. After all this time, I should anticipate Q's exuberance.

"Quinn!" Diane bounces up and down twice before she's enveloped by our mutual friend. "What are you doing here? Is Ryan here?"

"We're here." Ryan walks around Gil, carrying Lizzy in his arms. The toddler's bundled up like a pink Eskimo, complete with miniature shearling boots to her knees and faux fur trim on her parka. She twists in his arms, suddenly shy around strangers.

Ryan's wearing all black like a typical New Yorker. His hair is a little bit more salty at his temples under his hat. His dark eyes crinkle at the corners when he smiles.

Quinn is dressed as a lumbersexual from Brooklyn. It's kind of funny to see him standing next to John. Both men are attired in flannel, jeans and boots. John's boots sport scuffs and marks from work while Quinn's are perfectly polished. John wears a thick Carhartt coat. Quinn is in a navy cashmere peacoat. Even his knit cap sits at a jaunty angle, leaving his blond hair mostly exposed. The combination of coat and hat reminds me of a sailor.

Lumbersailor? I'll have to ask him if seamen is the new fashion trend. Or would that be lumberseamen? I laugh to myself. I'll have to share that with Selah later. I'll even give her permission to use it in one of her books.

"How long are you here?" Diane's eyes well up with tears.

Oh, boy. This is only part of the surprise. I told Quinn and John that shocking a hormonal woman is never a good idea, but they didn't listen. I hope she has tissues.

Ryan hands off Lizzy to Quinn. She reaches out her arms and says "Da-dee" as he takes her. Ryan gives Diane a big hug. "We're here for a week. New York misses you."

"Oh, I've missed you two so much. Happy Chanukah!"

Ryan beams at her. "Thanks for remembering us Jews. We're multi-denominational when it comes to Christmas. Our house is definitely on Santa's list, much to my mother's displeasure."

"Fine with the husband, but not Santa?" Gil chuckles.

"She's all about family traditions with the grandkids. Why do we need old St. Nick when we have eight nights of gifts."

Diane rubs her hand down Lizzy's back. "Of course she loves Little Lizzy. Well, not so little anymore."

"Speaking of not so little anymore." Quinn points at Diane's belly. "You're huge."

Only a gay man, well no, only Quinn, can get away with saying such things to a woman. Ever. He knows he can get away with it, too. Blunt is part of his charm.

"If you were blue, you could play Violet Beauregard in a production of *Willy Wonka*." He laughs at his own joke.

"Stop. I'm not that huge." Diane giggles.

"You polished off a triple scoop of ice cream and didn't even share," Tom says. I recognize him and his girlfriend from John's wedding last summer. I make the introductions all around.

"Quinn's one of my oldest friends," I explain.

"By old, she means we met as children. Toddlers, really."

It's my turn to laugh. "We met in college and we've earned these wrinkles."

"Wrinkles?" Quinn gasps. "Never!"

"Ryan's an amazing dermatologist," Diane tells her friends.

A driver honks his horn at us. I realize we're standing in the middle of the street. We move out of the way in a big clump, chatting all at the same time. Diane is now holding Lizzy's hand as we stroll. Lizzy still has her head tucked into Quinn's shoulder, but she holds a tight grip on Diane's finger.

"Do you think Ye Olde Carolers know the Wham Christmas song?" Quinn asks as the singers break into "Jingle Bells."

"I'd take some Mariah Carey over another round of 'Silent Night'." Diane suggests.

"Oh, I only like her song that was in *Love, Actually*," I say. "It's–"

"Your favorite movie." Gil and Quinn finish my sentence.

"Oh, I love that movie," Hailey agrees. "'God Only Knows' is a great song, too."

We run through a list of our favorite songs and scenes in the movie, becoming instant friends.

John taps away on his phone, oblivious to the conversation. I feel my phone vibrate in my coat pocket and take it out. I respond to his text, fighting a smile while I do it.

"Look at all this bearded goodness!"

The voice can only belong to my other best friend, Selah. I lift my eyes to spot her dark hair a dozen feet away. She's staring at John and Tom with a grin on her face. Standing beside her, Kai, her fiancé, is sporting a nice level of George Clooney style scruff. They got engaged this past summer, but I suspect they might be one of those couples that stays engaged for years. Or elope, and not tell anyone. I covertly eye their fingers for wedding bands, but find none. I love weddings, but who am I to talk? Gil and I have no plans to get married.

"Damn. It's a real live lumbersexual convention right here on the sidewalk." Selah purrs.

John visibly bristles at her words.

"Oh, Paul Bunyan, I don't mean you. You're the real thing. All seven feet of you." She teases him good-naturedly.

Even Hailey and Diane laugh at her nickname for John.

"Why didn't I come up with that one?" Hailey mumbles to her friend.

"Holy cats, you've procreated." Selah's eyes focus on Diane's belly. "You lucky, lucky woman."

Diane looks up at John and back at Selah in confusion.

"We haven't met. I'm Selah, the obnoxious friend." She sticks out her hand.

"Oh, I've heard all about you." Diane shakes her hand and adds, "All good things."

Selah's laugh is deep and throaty. "Then you haven't been talking to Quinn."

I observe our little group. Selah's right about the facial hair. Gil has started growing his winter beard. He'll shave it before the spring semester starts. Along with Kai, Quinn sports more scruff than usual. Only Ryan is clean-shaven. I guess beards are taking over the world.

Selah hugs Ryan and gives Quinn a half hug so she doesn't squish Lizzy. It's the closest ever Selah's come to holding her. I laugh as Lizzy lets go of Diane's finger to grab the fringe on Selah's cape/poncho. Despite her overstated dislike of children, Selah smiles and tickles Lizzy's nose with more fringe, causing the girl to giggle and lean in for more.

"When did you arrive?" I ask Kai. We might all live in Portland, but we rarely find time to get together. Kai spends a lot of time in Africa and travels the world for his non-profit work, taking Selah with him when she's not teaching.

"Yesterday. Selah finished her grades and we drove up in the evening."

"Are you settled in the house?" I'm happiest when my little cabin on the beach is filled with my favorite people.

"We are," Selah says. "We even brought a tree with us over on the ferry. Kai strapped it to the top of the car like he's a Norse God. I swear he lifted the thing with one arm."

She may notice other men, hell, we all notice good looking men like John and Tom, you'd have to be blind not to, but her heart is firmly held in the hands of Kai. He might even give the island guys a run for handsome. I know for a fact he looks amazing in a suit.

"Did he chop it down himself?" John asks. If it were John's tree, the answer would be yes. Knowing Kai, he bought the most expensive tree on the lot. I hope it fits in my living room.

Christmas at my beach cabin with my closest friends is my gift to myself this year. Even if our Christmas is a few days early so everyone can make it. We'd asked Ben and Jo to join us, but they're spending the holidays in Florida with her family. As Jo put it, it's the last chance to go to Disney World with sullen teens, and who wants to miss out on that fun. Selah's comments on their trip involved the words "sea of germs" and "hell portal."

"Baby, it's cold outside," she sing-says to the group. "I've done the strolling part of this evening, now how about some sipping?"

She's right about the cold. I tuck my plaid scarf tighter around my neck. Sitting on the bluff, Langley is exposed to the wind. A few flurries dance through the air.

"We have dinner plans." John drapes his arm around Diane. They stop walking, so we all stop.

"We do?" she asks

"I made reservations at Cafe Langley."

"You did?"

"I did." He smiles down at her.

"We have plans, too." Tom interrupts.

"Are you joining us?" Diane asks the group.

Tom and John exchange looks.

"No, um, our plans are separate. I've had enough festiveness for one evening." Tom gives Hailey a cautious look. He's normally so cocky and self-assured.

I don't know him well, but if I had to guess, he wants Hailey all to himself for the rest of the evening.

"Watch out for the mistletoe. The town is a minefield. Covered with the stuff." John points above our heads.

Gil rubs his hands together, a devilish glint in his eye. "I say we take full advantage of it. What say you, Maggie May?"

My old nickname always makes me swoon. I rise up on my tiptoes to kiss him. It's a soft, sweet kiss that ends too soon.

Gil scans the storefronts. "You owe me ten, no wait, twelve kisses."

I don't question his math. "Challenge accepted."

After saying goodbye and wishing us all merry Christmases, the two couples split off and walk in opposite directions down the crowded street.

Another surprise is waiting for Diane at the restaurant. I smile, knowing I did something really nice for John and his wife. After all, this season is about giving.

DIANE

John isn't a reservation and fancy dinner kind of guy. Yet here we are at a white-cloth covered table at Cafe Langley, my favorite restaurant. Even more strange is they seated us at a table for four. It's packed in here tonight because of the event.

I'm about to ask him what's going on when I hear my mother's voice.

Rather than turn toward her, I stare at my husband. "What did you do?"

He grins at me, but worry dances in his eyes. "I brought home to you, since you can't really travel for Christmas."

"You're my home, John Day. Our home is at the beach. Together."

He softly kisses my cheek, his beard tickling my skin. "I know, but I can't replace your parents."

"Hey sweetheart." My dad is standing next to the table now, wearing a Nordic sweater in a reindeer pattern. His bald head shines in the candlelight.

"Honey?" Mom asks, sounding worried. Her hair is shorter

than the last time I saw her, but still a warm brown with high-lights. Her face is thinner, too.

Tears spill down my cheeks as I stand up. "You're here."

I'm stunned stupid. "How?"

I hug both my parents as I cry. I'm not even sure why I'm crying.

Hormones? Probably.

Sentimental mush? Probably.

Realizing how much I've missed my mom? Definitely.

I'm now a blubbering mess in the middle of the restaurant. Not sobbing, but I do need to blow my nose soon or I'll get snot all over my mother's cashmere sweater.

"John called us and invited us to come out to visit you. He made all the arrangements and got his lovely friends Maggie and Gil to pick us up at the airport. She was there to get her friends from the city and brought two cars. Turns out we were all on the same flight. Everything worked out perfectly."

I gape at my husband. "You planned all this? To surprise me?"

His love shines in his eyes. Making me tear up even more, he hands me a bandana to blow my nose. He knows me so well. I blow my nose loudly, not caring I sound like an elephant, and wipe my eyes.

My mother hugs me again, wrapping her cashmere-covered arms around me from the side. "We're so happy to be here with you."

I nod, trying not to blubber again. Instead, I blow my nose once more. Exhaling a deep breath, I smile at the three people I love most in the world.

"You are all in so much trouble for keeping this a secret from me." My stern expression falters immediately. I'm too happy to fake it. "I love you so much."

John tucks me into his side and kisses the top of my head. "I love you."

He doesn't need to embellish those words. Those three are enough.

I stare up into his dark eyes. My stoic man who had closed himself off to love after loss. Even though the first time we met he yelled at me and accused me of being a burglar, there was something about him. I didn't know it then, but he'd captured my heart from that first day. Not that I was ready for him or a relationship. For a while, he was my only friend on the island. Now he's my best friend and my everything.

I get teary again thinking about how much I love him. I inhale and exhale a deep breath.

"Let's sit." I take the lead and settle into my seat at the table. Despite eating ice cream not that long ago, I'm hungry again. I could totally eat a big bowl of pasta.

John's arm drapes across the back of my chair. His familiar heat is comforting. The feel of his fingers playing with the ends of my hair grounds me. The tears seem to have faded for now.

I'm still stunned he surprised me with my parents. My own gift for him feels inadequate with this grand gesture. I know after the baby comes, he'll need guy time. He'll fret and worry over both of us, to his own detriment. Mom and my grandmother have both agreed to come out to help. John's aunt is close and a couple of his cousins have volunteered to help us. It takes a village, or in this case an island, to care for a baby.

That's why I bought him and Tom a trip to go fishing in Alaska next summer. The trick will be getting him to go. Tom's going to help out with that part. John'll listen to him. At least I hope so.

"What are you smiling about?" John asks.

I give him a sly grin. "Payback."

He frowns. "Are you mad?"

"Not at all." I squeeze his thigh. "I just hate being outdone when it comes to gifts."

Dad chuckles and lifts up his menu, blocking his face and

muffling his voice. "Son, you're never going to win. These women get competitive. You better watch out."

Mom sips her wine and nods. "Although, there aren't any losers in this game."

Mom's right. Trying to outdo each other with gifts is like trying to out-love each other. Nobody's a loser. Everyone wins. Tom and John go fishing for a week. I get a freezer full of salmon and halibut. Win-win.

CHAPTER 5

TOM

*H*ailey and I drive home together. She's nervous and fidgety in the truck, changing the radio station around after a minute or two into each song. Something's up.

When she reaches for the glove box, I swat her hand away and swerve into the opposite lane.

"What do you need in there?" I give her one of my flirtiest smiles. "Condoms a plenty at home."

"Ha ha. Are you hiding something?" She reaches for the handle and pulls, only it doesn't budge. Because it's locked. Her eyebrow lifts in question.

"I think it's jammed." I point out her window. "Was that a coyote?"

There is no coyote. I need a distraction.

She turns her head to look out the back window. When she faces me again, she squints to study me, but doesn't say anything.

I need to make it home and get her inside, before her death stare makes me blow everything. She can be scary when she puts on that face.

We bump along the dirt road to my house. When we reach the clearing, a few fat snowflakes hit the windshield.

"Ooh, it's snowing." She jumps out of the cab as soon as I put it in park. Tilting her head back, she slowly spins with her arms out. Snowflakes land and melt on her coat and scarf, disappearing almost instantly. I lean against the warm hood of the truck, watching her enjoy the first snow of the season.

A certainty swells up within me. I didn't really have a plan for proposing other than asking my grandmother for one of the family rings. I was stunned when she gave me the one Pops proposed with. Over time she upgraded and changed styles, but this is the one he picked out all those years ago when money was tight and their future endless.

The ring is more of a diamond covered band than one of those rings with a big hunk of rock. It's far from flashy or a big state-ment. Hailey isn't that type of woman anyway. She doesn't even really wear jewelry. Something simple with a story behind it will be perfect. I hope.

What do I know about rings and women? What if she wants a new ring and a big diamond? My heart begins to race. I could seriously blow this whole thing with the wrong ring.

"It's always magical." She sighs and opens her eyes. "What? Why are you staring at me like that?"

I inhale, trying to stuff my rising panic back down. Blowing out a slow, long exhale, I try to give her a confident grin. I feel anything, but confident right now. My palms are damp with sweat. Blood races in my ears. I try to take another breath, but my lungs won't cooperate. Black spots dot my vision. *What is going on?*

"Tom?" Hailey rushes over to me. "You've gone pale. Are you okay?"

Her voice sounds far away even though she is only a few inches from my face. Her hands cup my head. I attempt to focus on her eyes, but they keep going all soft and blurry.

"You look like you're going to pass out." She gives my head a little shake.

I can't answer her. Instead, I slump against the truck, sliding down until I'm sitting against the front passenger tire.

"Tom." Her voice is all muffled and tinny. "Put your head between your knees."

I do as she suggests, tilting forward to rest my head on my knees. Cold air and snow prickle against my exposed skin covered in a thin layer of sweat. I'm hot, but I shiver at the sensation. I practice breathing like it's a new thing for me.

"I'll be right back." Her boots stomp on the gravel in the direction of the house.

I've blown the moment big time. At least I didn't have the ring out before I almost passed out from nerves like a virgin on prom night. Not that I would know. I wasn't a virgin at prom.

When the world stops spinning, I lift my head. Snow sticks to the tarps and the pine trees across the yard. So much for just flurries tonight. I stare up at the falling flakes. They float and drift down on me. It's quiet and peaceful out here. I don't know where Hailey's gone to, but I think I can stand. I push off the ground. Things are still fuzzy, but the dizziness has passed.

Small yippy barks break the silence. It's not a coyote's high-pitched howl. It sounds like–

A tiny fur-ball careens around the front tire, barking at me. I'm sure he thinks he's fierce. Immediately, he's tugging on the leg of my jeans. The thing growls and chomps at the denim like he's going to take me down. It's like a chipmunk going after a bear.

I bend to pick him up, careful to avoid his mouth. He won't let go of my jeans, until I put my finger in the jaws of death to get him to release. His incredibly sharp teeth graze my skin a few times like tiny knives.

"Hey, fierce little—" I turn the pup over, "—little dude. What's up with the attack mode? You going to take me down?"

He squirms in my hands, wiggling himself around to chomp on my fingers or sleeve.

"Ouch! Now, you've got to stop that." I suck on my finger

where he's made contact. At least there's no blood. "Where did you come from? Whose evil puppy are you?"

He's not wearing a collar or tags. We're close enough to my sister's house that he could have escaped from there, but he would've had to walk through the woods to get here. I doubt he'd be able to make it.

I tuck him under my arm like a football, so he can't bite me. I open the door and unlock the glove box to get the ring. The puppy tugs on my coat sleeve. I drop him and the ring box on the floor of the truck. He immediately goes after the box. I'm not worried he can swallow it because it's bigger than his jaw, but he's got it between his teeth.

I try to grab the box. He thinks it's a game, scampering around in the truck. I lean in further to secure the ring, resting on my stomach across the seat to stop him before he gets himself wedged someplace I can't reach him.

"What are you doing?" Hailey returns. "I went to get you some water, but then I got distracted because I lost something in the house. Why are you lying face down in the truck?"

"Got you!" I make a final lunge for the puppy and wrap my hand around his belly. I shove back off the seat and onto my feet. Holding the tiny dog above my head in triumph, I forget he's holding the ring box in his teeth.

"Oh! You found Nameless." She sounds relieved. "What's that in his mouth?"

Oh, crap.

"Nameless?" I tuck him under my arm again and attempt to extract the cream velvet box before she can figure out what it is. Nameless growls and squirms, but unless I want to get bit again, he's not giving up his new toy.

"I, um, he's …" She stumbles over her words. Smiling she shouts, "Merry Christmas! I got you a puppy."

I stare at her in disbelief. "You got me a poodle puppy?"

Her smile is warm, but a little nervous. "He's a Labradoodle."

"You got me a dog." I take a few steps closer. Now we're inches apart. "You got us a dog."

She nods, her expression soft and full of love. "I did. You can name him, though. That's why I've been calling him Nameless."

I kiss her because I don't know what to say. I kiss her because I love her.

Nameless uses my distraction to bite my arm again.

I jerk back from Hailey, nearly dropping the puppy. I fumble, but save him from falling.

The box drops onto the ground.

I'm pretty sure my hand is bleeding.

She bends down to pick up the box. The velvet is soaked in puppy saliva. So gross. She holds it between two fingers. "What's this?"

My breath goes shallow again. Her own expression holds an edge of panic.

This is one of those fork in the road life moments.

I can toss the puppy at her, hoping she'll drop the box to save him, and then I can stuff the box in my pocket, denying everything.

Or I can man up, and do what I know I want.

I take the box and hand her the puppy. He stops squirming and settles into the crook of her arm. I swear he even gives me a smug look like he belongs there. If anyone is going to snuggle Hailey, it's going to be me. He's going to sleep on a dog bed. Downstairs.

My pulse races again, but I take a deep breath, calming myself.

I bend down on one knee, and look up at her. Her eyes shine with tears. I say a silent prayer that they're happy tears before speaking.

"Hailey King, I love you with my whole heart. Will you do me the honor of being my wife, my partner?" I open the box on the second try and present the ring to her.

She's nodding, but hasn't said yes. Snow swirls around and

sticks to her hair, even her lashes have a few flakes that slowly melt into the tears now running down her face.

The ground is cold so I stand up still holding the ring and its box. "Is that a yes?"

She nods again before kissing me. The memory of the cold snow and her warm mouth will stay with me always. I don't need a verbal yes. Her kiss tells me she's mine.

"I love you," she whispers against my mouth.

I slip the ring onto her finger and enclose her in my arms.

She's my world.

My love.

My future.

The puppy bites my arm. Again.

I think about building him a heated doghouse as I carry them both inside the house.

I hope you enjoyed this future glimpse into the lives of the characters from both my Modern Love Stories and Wingmen series.

If you enjoyed *Give and Take*, please check out the other novels and shorts in the series. For more of my writing, there's a reading order at the end of this book.

If you're already a Wingmen lover, check out *Small Town Scandal*.

If you're already a Modern Love Stories fan, *Happily Ever Now* (Lizzy's book) is in the works.

TWO WINGMEN AND A BABY

A WINGMEN SHORT

INTRODUCTION

This short originally appeared in the Red Hot Sizzle anthology. After writing a pregnant Diane in *Give and Take*, I knew I wanted to write a story of John and Tom, my two alpha wingmen, taking care of a little Baby Day. I love the image of John as a father and the affect a baby has on our Tom Cat.

Hold onto your ovaries because this short features John, Tom Cat, and sweet Baby Day.

Two alpha men can take care of a baby without anything crazy happening, right?

This short takes place after *Confessions of a Reformed Tom Cat* and overlaps with both *Anything but Love* and *Better Love*. Told in Tom's POV.

CHAPTER 1

The sound of screaming slaps me as soon as I open my truck's door in front of John's beach cabin.

I jump down and tense my legs. My blood begins to race as adrenaline fires. Fight or flight kicks in. I listen, trying to determine the source and which direction I should run.

The sound shifts and becomes wailing. Very loud wailing.

No one is getting murdered or attacked. No one is dying.

Someone is crying.

It's the baby.

From inside the house.

Wow, she's got some impressive lungs.

I should've brought ear plugs. For me and John.

Opening the front door, I brace myself as the volume increases tenfold. I'm cradling a six pack of beer on top of one of Dan's pizza boxes. Both nearly crash to the ground when I reach the kitchen.

A few feet away in the living room, Baby Day is squawking her little lungs out. Crying Baby Day isn't anything new, so that's not what makes me almost drop my beer and pizza.

Baby Day, aka Alene, is currently sitting inside Babe's dog crate.

Basically she's in a baby kennel.

Not that there is such a thing as a kennel for babies. That's probably frowned upon by parents.

I'm pretty sure in a pinch you could use a dog kennel.

Not that anyone would. Except John, evidently.

All this is passing through my head while I quickly set down the goods and stride across the large room to rescue the baby from the baby trap.

Okay, so I might be exaggerating.

I know. Go figure.

It's not like she's locked in a metal cage. The crate is more like a rectangular tent. Not unlike a portable play pen. I can see how from a baby's perspective they're the same thing.

I scoop up Alene under her arms and she screams in my face.

She's not the first woman to do it.

Her little fist flails and thumps my cheek.

Not the first girl to slap me either.

In fact, she's the second woman today to be mad at me—who I know about. There could be more. With a fiancée, three sisters, a mom, and a grandmother, it's highly likely one of them is upset with me on any given day. It's a gift and a curse.

Hailey and I got into a stupid argument this morning. She brought up the wedding and I suggested eloping to avoid "the monkey suit circus."

Sure, in hindsight I can see where I went off the rails with such a comment. Unless you're certain your bride to be wants a circus themed wedding, never bring monkeys into any conversations about her special day.

Hindsight sucks compared to knowing when to keep my mouth shut. Something I'm still working on. Gotta learn to crawl before walking wisdom and all. I love Hailey more than anything in the world. She's my life. Doesn't stop me from saying stupid things.

Speaking of crawling ...

As self-punishment, I'm now holding a crying baby. Not really. I'm not a masochist.

John invited me over to keep him company this afternoon. "Company" is guy code for back-up reinforcements. In our younger days, that would've meant being his wingman to pick up women.

Now it's something entirely different, although there are still women involved. One miniature woman in particular, who is still crying in my face.

"Hey now, Baby Day. It's me. Tom." I point to my face. "We're buddies. Remember?"

From truck to baby holding has taken about two minutes. Uncle Tom to the rescue!

She hiccups and her crying dies down. Her whole head is red in anger.

It's easy to see all of her head because she's completely bald. Even at six months. Shouldn't babies have hair by now? Diane swears there's peach fuzz, but you have to be in the right light to see it. As a blond, I look like a little old bald man in most of my baby and little kid pictures. Maybe Alene will take after me.

Wait, I'm not saying there's any reason she would. For the record, Diane shot me down way before I could fully unleash the Tom Cat charms on her.

"Where's your dad? Huh?" I shift Alene's solid weight so she's sitting on my arm. Tears still run down her cheeks but she's stopped shrieking like a banshee. Her little, fat hand grips the front of my flannel shirt. I pull the fabric away from my chest to protect my chest chairs. I don't have much, but that phrase about having someone by the short hairs has a whole new meaning when it's a freakishly strong baby hand doing the pulling.

Our girl has a grip on her. I've learned that one from too many painful experiences. She can also kick her ham-legs hard enough to make a grown man see stars. Trust me. I speak from firsthand knowledge.

"Daddy's coming!" John rushes into the room. The button on his jeans is undone and he's holding a folded newspaper.

"I bet that's what you tell Diane all the time." I tuck my chin close to Alene's head and whisper, "Your daddy is a pervert."

"Thomas Clifford Donnely, don't be telling my daughter that kind of thing." John bellows and storms over to reclaim his daughter.

I step away and shield the baby from him. "Don't interrupt us. We were having a nice moment after I rescued her from Babe's crate."

"The crate?" He falters and stops. "She was in the crate again? Diane's going to kill me."

"What were you doing? You can't leave a baby unattended." I scold him like I don't know what he was doing in the bathroom with a newspaper. Sometimes my best friend is an old man.

"I didn't leave her unattended. Babe was with her."

I scope out the room for John's yellow lab. A tail thumps the floor from behind the couch near the door to the deck. "You left the dog in charge?"

He rubs his neck. "I had to go to the bathroom. I had the door open. Everything was fine. I could hear her chattering away like she does. I was almost done with my business when she started fussing. I couldn't exactly get up in the middle of it."

"Your fly is still down." I gesture around his middle. "Why didn't you take her in there with you? You could have laid a towel in the tub and put her down in there."

He zips up and goes to the sink to wash his hands. "I don't know. Something feels wrong about having her in there with me. Plus, she was happily playing in her baby fun zone when I stepped away. How did she even get over to the crate?"

We both look between Alene and the distance from her fun zone to the crate. It's at least five feet away.

"Are you crawling?" I ask the baby. She blinks at me, a few tears still stuck in her lashes. She smiles, but doesn't give up her secrets. Typical woman.

"She rolls over and also scoots like she's doing the Worm. I guess it's possible."

"Your days of pooping alone are over for now, my friend." I slap John on the back with my free hand.

Alene reaches out for her dad and I reluctantly hand her over. She grins at him and immediately goes for his beard.

I laugh at John's grimace when she pulls too hard. "Guess all chicks are unable to resist the power of the beard."

He frowns and holds her away from his body. "Speaking of pooping."

A distinct odor hits me. "Maybe it's just gas?"

We both watch Alene's face. I don't know about John, but I'm holding my breath, too. Her little forehead crinkles and the loudest fart noise escapes her diaper. She giggles.

Both Babe and I jump in surprise. Babe's got a "don't blame me" look in his eyes. He paws at the door to go outside.

I'm happy to let him out and let John take over. "Good plan. Let's escape while we can."

Babe runs out the door, shoving his dog shoulders through the narrow gap before I can even open it fully. He bounds down the deck steps and onto the beach. His tail sticks up above the tall grass before he disappears.

John holds Alene above his head and sniffs her butt. When he lowers her, she grunts. He lifts her, and she giggles. Lower. Grunt. Raise. Giggle.

A smile spreads across my face. Who can resist baby giggles?

Not this guy.

"Does she need to be changed?" I'm still holding the door handle and have one foot resting on the threshold.

"I can't tell. Maybe." He sniffs again.

My laughing begins at a chuckle before it escalates to full blown belly laughs.

"What's so funny?" Both John's and Alene's eyes are focused on me. I swear she lifts her eyebrow exactly like her dad. This makes me laugh harder. I'm halfway out the door and trip over my own feet. Sprawling on the deck, my laughter subsides. Babe runs over to me and licks my face. I swat him away and he flops down on the decking next to my head, presenting his belly for a rub.

John and Alene stand in the door above me. I cup my hand over my eyes to see them in the bright sunshine.

Yep, she definitely has her dad's eyebrow arch. His dark eyes, too. Thankfully she takes after her mother's beauty. No beard, no mustache.

The thought brings back my laughter. When I can breathe again, I answer him. "A couple of years ago you were chasing girls butts, not sniffing them."

He tilts his head to the side. Baby Day mirrors him. It's a little uncanny, to be honest.

"Well, two years ago you weren't making out with a dog and giving each other mutual belly rubs."

Babe's paw is resting on my bare skin that's exposed between my shirt and my jeans.

I get my feet under myself and jump up. "I've seen you let him lick you on the lips, so you're not one to talk."

When I stand, Alene extends her arms toward me.

"Same with you and Nameless." John hands her to me. "You ever going to pick a name for your puppy?"

"Nameless is a name. He answers to it."

"He bite you lately?"

I rub my arm in memory. "No, the puppy bitey phase seems to have passed. He growled at me from my side of the bed the other night. Hailey thought it was cute and joked I should just sleep on the couch."

John snorts. "How'd that go over?"

"The puppy spent the night in his crate. Downstairs." Damn dog. "He's more her dog than mine. Follows her everywhere and lies at her feet in worship."

Hailey gave him to me for Christmas. She said he was better than a fish, which had been my idea.

The dog ruined my big proposal plans.

Let's not re-live that night again.

What counts is that it all turned out just fine in the end. Hence the monkey and circus comment getting me in trouble this morning.

Still haven't set a date or really planned anything.

Baby steps.

No pun intended.

Another impressive sound escapes Alene's diaper.

"I'm ninety-percent certain that wasn't a simple fart." I hold her out in front of me. She kicks her feet and squirms.

"We have a house rule. Whoever is holding her or is closer when she needs changing, wins."

"Wins? Wins what?"

John backs away. "You're it!"

"You aren't seriously going to make me change a diaper?" I try to give the baby back to him. He runs away. Like a little girl.

No offense, Alene.

He flings a diaper bag out the door. It lands at my feet. "You have more experience than I do. All those Donnely nieces and nephews running around the island. At some point your sisters probably made you change a diaper."

"Have you met my sisters? They make me sit at the kids' table." I made a face at Alene and she smiled, happy as a piglet in shit. "You want me to change her out here in the open?"

"Better than unleashing the kraken inside the house." He closes the door and gestures for me to get on with it.

"The kraken?" I ask, staring at Alene.

John's voice is slightly muted by the glass. "That's what we call it after one memorable explosion."

I shudder.

Eyeing Alene, I roll back my shoulders. I can do this. I've changed maybe five diapers in my life. How bad can it be?

I gag.

For the third time.

"What are you feeding this baby?"

I have the diaper changing pad-blanket-tarp spread out on the deck. Alene lies in the middle of it. Her baby jumpsuit is open and pushed out of the way of whatever toxic sludge is making my eyes water.

John opens the door and leans against the jamb. Smartly supervising from a safe distance. "Breast milk and a little rice cereal."

"Okay, then you need to seriously change Diane's diet." I'd hold my nose but I need both hands free. Instead I try breathing through my mouth like I do when I gut fish.

If I'm being honest, gutting fish is a lot less disgusting than what this innocent baby has in her diaper.

I'll skip the details, but it takes a lot of wipes to deal with the bio-hazard. Alene laughs and tries to hold her feet the entire time.

I gag again. "You should've named her Helena."

John glares. "I know you think Helena Day is hysterical, but puns don't make good names."

"I meant after your aunt." No I didn't. "Come on. Hell in a Day is an awesome baby name. She could grow up to be a superhero or in a roller derby with that name."

"She can pick her own derby name." He says this without even questioning Alene doing roller derby. If she ends up with his giant height and Hulk shoulders, she could be a derby queen someday.

I wrestle a clean diaper on Alene as she squirms. The past couple of minutes have felt like trying to catch Nameless as he runs around the house with one of my shoes. I'm exhausted and I might be sweating. I wipe my brow with the back of my hand that hasn't been cleaning up fluids.

"Does she always poop this much?" The dirty diaper must weigh at least two pounds.

John laughs, but doesn't move to help. "It's good practice for you."

"Practice for what? Dealing with shit?" I snicker. "I mean actual shit, you know."

"I figure now that you have a dog, that's probably already true." He nods at the tiny human currently playing with her own toes. "You know what I'm talking about."

"No way. Not happening any time soon. We're taking care of that."

"What are you waiting for?"

I blink up at him before deflecting. "You grow a vagina? Cause you sure are sounding like one of Hailey's girlfriends right now."

Alene must think this is a terrible idea because she begins fussing. I quickly snap her jumpsuit closed and pick her up.

"Don't worry. I was kidding about your dad." I raise my voice into a falsetto. "He'd make the ugliest woman ever. Wouldn't he? Yes, he would."

I'm rewarded with a drooly grin. I continue smiling at her and doing my best Mrs. Doubtfire impression. "Who's a lucky girl she looks exactly like her beautiful mommy?"

She makes a happy chirping sound right before she head butts me. I bite my tongue. Pain shoots through my mouth and a string of expletives follow.

"Motherfucker!" I swipe my tongue over my lip expecting to taste the metallic bite of copper.

"Language!" John grabs her and covers her ears.

"She's a baby. She can't understand anything we're saying. Have you heard yourself? You'll be lucky if her first word isn't fuck."

"Shut up, asshole." His eyes widen. "Fuck."

I chuckle as I pick up the diaper and huge pile of wet wipes. There are at least ten. "I'm not sure how many you normally use."

"That seems about right. There's a baggie in there you can put everything in."

I pull out what looks like a doggy poop bag. It even smells nice. "Fancy."

"Diane's mom sent them." He shrugs.

"These should have a skull and crossbones on them. Or the nuclear waste symbol." I crack myself up.

Hey, being easily amused makes life a lot easier to deal with, especially during the tough times.

"She sends a lot of stuff." I eye the pile of toys stuffed into baskets and totes in their living room behind him.

"She takes her grandmother role very seriously. Because she can't be here all the time, she sends things. Weekly. We're going to need a bigger cabin soon."

John's mom died years ago. He's not close with his dad. Unlike my immediate family of siblings and countless nieces and nephews, John's family is pretty small. He sees his aunt and uncle a lot. His aunt Helen has happily taken over grandmother duties. She'll babysit or bring over a casserole every day if John would let her.

"Where is Diane today, anyway?"

He rubs his beard, then reaches for a chubby little hand, and kisses the back. "She woke up this morning and said she needed a day to be Diane and not Mommy."

I furrow my brow. "What does that mean?"

"I'm not really sure, but there were tears. Lots of tears."

We meet each other's stares and widen our eyes.

"Oh." Tears are never good. Unless they're "happy tears." Whatever those are. Honestly, even those are a little scary. A sobbing woman can break a man in a matter of minutes. When it comes to dealing with our emotions, men are most definitely the weaker sex.

A hormonal, crying woman? Something to be feared and coddled. Best from a distance. Men are fixers. We'll fix what's broken, tinker with what works fine, and sometimes mess things up just to fix them later and be a hero. We like concrete solutions. We're simple like that.

This is the reason why I have the florist's number in my phone. Sometimes the solution is flowers and pizza from Sal's. Sometimes I stop and get a bottle of Hailey's favorite wine. There are times when I need all three, plus chocolate. Those times I do a drive by delivery and go hang out at The Dog House until I get the all clear.

I'm not a coward. I'm smart enough to know that sometimes women need to be alone. Or with other women. Hen house without the rooster. Fine by me. Breaks my heart to see Hailey or any woman I love in tears.

Not afraid to admit that. Not in the least.

"Where'd she go?" I swing the full baggie. Realizing what I'm holding, and drop it.

"She called a friend and they went over to town. Last minute spa day and shopping. Lunch."

Town can mean anything from the ferry dock to Seattle and beyond. "Off island is good. Right?"

"She mumbled something about wearing clothes that aren't covered in someone else's bodily fluids and not being a cow. At that point, she was crying so hard, I couldn't really understand her. I just hugged her and told her she's beautiful."

"Smart."

We both nod, then stand in silence staring at Alene who is holding John's finger. I'm pretty sure we're both thinking the same thing. Someday the little person in his arms is going to turn into a woman— a complicated, beautiful creature who will befuddle us and whom we will protect from pain with everything we have.

She already has both of us by the short hairs of our hearts. If you lean into it, it doesn't hurt. It's only painful if you try to pull away.

"I need to feed this one. Mind if I do that before we eat?"

"Pizza's cold and the beer is probably warm." I walk ahead of him, tossing the diaper bag on the couch before heading to the garage to dispose of the baggie.

Returning to the kitchen, I find John opening the microwave to heat up the pizza. Alene perches in his arms like a small supervisor. She misses nothing, and claps when he reaches for the bottle warmer.

"I'll put the beer in the fridge for a bit." I open the door and am greeted with baggies of breast milk. A lot of them. My mouth gapes open. I can understand why Diane feels like a cow. She's a freaking dairy queen.

"If you can't find room for the beer in there, try the one in the garage."

I notice he doesn't call it the beer fridge anymore. Shifting a few things around, I'm able to lay most of the bottles flat. I stuff two into the freezer for a couple of minutes.

John sits in a rocking recliner and feeds the baby while I sip on my own bottle.

The two of them are in a bubble. If we lived in a cartoon world, little baby chicks and hearts would be circling his head while she pats his scruffy face and drinks her lunch.

I sit alone on the sofa and feel like I'm watching a stranger. My wingman, my best friend from our teens is now a dad. All six foot too many inches of bearded, flannel wearing, grumbling guy is grinning at his baby, the spawn of his loins, like he's never seen anything more beautiful in the world.

"What's happened to us?" I don't mean to say it out loud.

"We grew up."

Alene pops off her bottle, dribbling milk down her chin as she twists to look at me. I swear she ducks her chin and flirts. Can't say I blame her. I have that effect on women of all ages.

"She likes deep voices," John laughs.

"You are so screwed." I shake my head.

"Just you wait until you have your own."

I choke on air.

CHAPTER 3

While the baby naps, we eat pizza and shoot the shit. I have a second beer and John has his first.

"I can't have more than one in case I need to drive somewhere." His eyes wander over to the baby monitor. The light reassures us it's on and working.

I hear familiar lyrics from my own childhood.

"How long have we been listening to baby songs?" I point at the speaker in case John needs clarity. "Are these the original lyrics? I always sang it 'do your balls hang low.' Huh."

He grabs the remote and switches playlists. "About a half hour. Happens to me all the time now. I took Diane's Jeep yesterday and found myself singing along to John Jacob Jinglelheimer Schmidt."

"You still know all the words? That's impressive." I give him a semi-sarcastic thumbs up.

"It's basically the name over and over again."

"I bet you rocked it like you did Taylor Swift."

"How'd you know about... oh, right. Diane and Hailey are friends."

I nod. "No secrets."

For a few minutes we settle into a comfortable quiet, sipping our beer and eating slices of pizza.

"Speaking of gossip, you talk to Dan lately?" I ask.

He shakes his head no. "Why?"

"When I stopped in to get the pizza, there was woman there."

John stares at me. "So?"

"I didn't recognize her. She was fancy. High heels and painted nails."

"Like a hooker?"

"Hookers are fancy?" I shoot him a glare. "No, Seattle fancy. She glared at Dan while he ignored her from behind the counter."

"How do you know he was ignoring her?"

"He wouldn't look over at the tables. At all. I even moved around in front of the counter so he'd have to look in that direction. Nope. Kept his head down."

"Spurned lover?"

"Spurned something, but I doubt she's an ex. Too hoity for him."

As far as we both know, Dan lives the life of a monk. Never see him with a woman. Hell, we rarely see him outside his pizza place. Other than the trip to the San Juans last year for John's bachelor weekend with the Kelso brothers, we don't socialize with him much at all. I know Erik Kelso is on some local business council with him, but I get the feeling Dan keeps to himself for reasons he also keeps to himself.

He works six days a week, lives alone, and that's about all we've got. The man can talk your ear off about wood-burning ovens, best types of wood, and area farms, but ask him something personal and he clams up. I know he's not from the island because he opened the pizzeria about five years ago when he moved here. His house sits on a high bluff overlooking Holmes Harbor. Rumors say he spent a lot of money on it. Where he got that kind of money is anyone's guess. He hates big business and banks. If someone ever brings up chain restaurants or franchises, watch out. He'll give an earful about the evils of corporate America squashing the dreams of the honest small businesses.

He's kind of an odd duck.

Hailey and Diane think he's hot. They call him a silver fox, whatever that is. I think he must put something in his pizza dough that's affected their brains. Or it's the jalapeño and pineapple nonsense they love that has both convinced that Dan's quiet loner status equals romantic movie hero.

"Strange indeed. As long as he keeps making great pizza, what, or who he does, is none of my business."

"Yeah. Just odd, that's all." I shrug.

The baby monitor comes to life, letting us know Baby Day is awake and demanding our servitude.

John sets down his beer. "I'll get her. You want to take a walk? She likes to check out the neighborhood and wave at her admirers in the afternoon."

I wipe my hands on my jeans. "I'll get the stroller ready."

"You sure? Last time you gave yourself a blood blister trying to open it." He dodges the balled up paper towel I throw at his head.

"Damn you and your overly sophisticated baby gear." I'm laughing. He's right. The stroller is one of these deluxe deals where you push one button and it unfolds like magic. I rub my thumb against my index finger at the painful memory.

I open another beer and pick up the stroller. I pop open the queen's carriage outside the front door. It even comes with convenient cupholders for mommy's wine or daddy's beer. These designers think of everything.

John and Alene come out. Babe follows behind. Baby Day's bundled up in a pink fleece jacket. In her hand she holds a hat that I'm guessing should be on her head. Currently she's using it to hit her dad's shoulder. Everything is a weapon around her. Understanding clicks about why parents have to lock down everything and hide the sharp objects. These micro-ninjas are dangerous.

I catch John staring at the stroller.

"Are you using the cupholder for your beer?"

"Yeah. That's so cool they added them for the parents." I pick up the bottle and take a swig. "You want me to grab you one?"

"That's not for beer, you doofus. It's for bottles, baby bottles and sippy cups."

"You mean those wine sippy cups women like?"

"No," he grumbles. "Although Diane has one of those."

"So does Hailey. Her mom got her a set for the hot tub."

Babe wanders along the sandy shoulder, nose to the ground. I stroll beside John and Princess Alene. We create the world's smallest parade as we walk down the road. This time of year, things are quiet down here at the beach. It's sunny and warm for early October and a few of John's neighbors are puttering around their properties. Sure enough, Alene waves and smiles at everyone we pass.

Occasionally Babe walks beside the carriage, even putting his nose close to Alene.

"Does he always check on her?"

"I'm telling you, he's a great baby sitter. I totally trust him."

"Except for earlier."

"Don't tell Diane. She worries too much. I want her to be able to have breaks and fun with her friends without thinking I'm too incompetent to take care of my own daughter."

His daughter.

The pinging in my chest returns. I rub the spot, but the twinge doesn't go away.

"You're the most competent man under forty I know."

"Who else do you hang out with? The Kelsos? Yeah, not a lot of competition for being a real adult with them."

"Erik's doing all right."

John bursts out in laughter. "Nothing like your ass going viral to make you grow up."

With a chuckle I join him. "Yeah, but the calendar was my idea. Pretty brilliant if you ask me."

"A calendar wasn't exactly on your mind when you threatened to streak down Anthes street."

"I still think we should do a naked sprint down First. Raise money for another charity. Prostate cancer's been done. Maybe testicular cancer? Save the balls?"

John rolls his neck. "Damn, when are you going to grow out of this need to be naked outside?"

"Never?" Being naked outside is amazing. Unless there are raccoons and rangers involved. "You have to admit last summer's snipe hunt was pretty awesome."

With his eyes closed, John shakes his head. His voice is low when he speaks. "Damn, I can't believe that was only a year ago."

I glance at Princess Pea-shoot's chubby arm hanging over the side of her stroller. "A lot's changed."

John ducks his head to see her. A happy laugh rewards him. "I can't imagine my world without her."

I trip over a pebble.

"Don't give me shit about it, Donnely."

After righting myself, I catch up to him. "Never. I've seen the same thing happen with my sisters and their babies. I think babies must emit some sort of special chemical. Hailey is always sniffing baby heads like an addict."

He rubs his jawline. "You two ever talk about kids?"

A conversation from April right after Alene's birth echoes in my head. "Hailey talks about starting a family."

"Just Hailey?"

"I usually change the subject. Between Lori and Diane, her friends are giving her baby fever. We're not ready. We live together. We have Nameless. We're already a family. Isn't that enough?"

What I don't say is that sometimes I fear I'm not enough. Can't I have her all to myself for a while before I have to share her body with an invader? Before someone else becomes the number one in her life? I love being the focus of her love. I don't want to split her attention. How ridiculous would it be to be jealous of a baby? I don't want to be that guy.

After remaining silent for a minute or two, John responds. "I get that."

We continue in silence to the end of the road.

I'm happy. Damn, content even. I don't like change or the unknown. I've worked as a welder for over a decade because it's easy and I know what to expect. I live on land owned by my family for generations. Hell, I didn't have any real responsibilities in my twenties. Not even a pet fish. Then Hailey King crashed back into my world and I realized how much I'd been missing by not growing up. I love her beyond my imagination. However, after proposing within the first year we dated, I'm stalling on setting a date to make her mine forever.

As we turn back from the channel to the lagoon, realization hits me.

I like being engaged. I like knowing she's mine.

But I'm in limbo again, living in the status quo because it's comfortable.

Thing needs to change.

John and I are sprawled on the couch, watching college football when Diane gets home. It's dark out and we've only turned on the lights in the kitchen, leaving the room in shadows from the blue glow of the flat screen.

John jumps up and greets her with a hug. I feel like a creeper watching as he kisses the top of her head, then tilts her chin up. When he goes in for the kiss, I focus on the television and the sleeping baby on my chest. They softly whisper to each other for a few minutes.

Leaning away from John's arms, Diane spots Alene asleep on me. "Look at you, Tom Cat. Hold still."

Before I can do anything, which isn't much given the sleeping baby, she snaps a pic with her phone. Typing away on her screen, her smile widens.

"Please tell me you didn't post that to Facebook," I whisper.

"I'm not that cruel. No, I texted it to Hailey."

Great. "You're a menace, you know that right? Don't give Hailey any ideas." My annoyance is mostly an act. Hailey's eyes get all dreamy whenever she sees me holding a baby. There's a look she gets I've learned to recognize which often leads to her jumping me as soon as we're alone. I not so secretly love it when she takes the initiative. Diane's doing us a sexual favor.

After setting her phone on the counter, Diane quietly moves to stand in front of me. She leans down and softly kisses the top of Alene's head. "Want me to put her to bed?"

"Nah, it's okay. She's not bothering me." I spread my hand out on Alene's small back. Her body is so warm and cozy, like a sweet smelling, onesie wearing hot water bottle.

"Tom, she can't get used to sleeping on a man's chest again. We'll never get her to fall asleep in her crib."

"Again?" I raise an eyebrow.

Diane's eyes cut to John and I see him brush his hand up his neck. "Yeah. Softie over there would pick her up if she so much as frowned, then hold her until she fell asleep again. She used to hold onto his beard even in her sleep. We got a squirrel stuffie. The tail makes a nice replacement."

Instead of teasing John, which would be so easy to do right now, something pings in my chest. Like a rubber band hitting my sternum, there is a little sting and I want to rub it away except I can't because there is a baby cover the spot.

"Shut up, Tom." John cuts me off from the insult Diane lobbed to me.

To ease the ache behind my ribs, I go for it anyway. "I always did think your beard was harboring some woodland creatures."

He groans. "And there it is."

I chuckle, which shakes my chest and Alene stirs, scrunching up her face and gripping my shirt. She manages to trap a few chest hairs in her tiny fist. It's painful enough to make my eyes water, but I don't want to disturb her. I try exhaling away the pain.

Diane is hovering over me, ready to pounce on her daughter the second the baby moves again. I can see down her shirt and normally I'd instinctually check out her boobs, but I don't. She's a mom now. Those are sacred boobs. At least for now. You see a baby attached and nursing, it kind of changes the way you see a woman's breasts.

An image of topless Hailey flashes through my mind. Hailey's small perfect breasts with the most beautiful nipples the shade of peonies. Yeah, I learned the name of those flowers. Had to so I can I order them over the phone for her all the time. In fact, I had my grandmother plant some around our house.

I close my eyes briefly to capture the image of my favorite breasts in existence. Only when I imagine them there's a small mouth attached to a nipple, suckling while a tiny hand touches the soft skin I know so well.

My body jerks with shock. This time Alene's eyelashes flutter before her brown eyes flash open. She doesn't cry. It's more of a grunt, like a little piglet. She stares at me with an intensity that flays me open. There is a knowing and understanding in her eyes that tells me she's a minuscule mind reader. Her fingers tighten over my heart.

She knows all.

A vision of a petite Hailey with my eyes and dimple flashes into my head.

I blink a few times.

My own daughter.

No, we'd be better off with boys. Three of them.

Three?

Where did that come from?

My pulse speeds up and I can feel sweat breaking out on the back of my neck.

A little hand taps my chin, telling me it'll be all right.

I capture Alene's hand before she can jab or poke out an eye. Kissing her palm, I continue to stare into her all-knowing eyes.

Maybe we'll start with one and build up to three.

I survived the kraken today.

I'm invincible.

The twinge in my chest goes away and a warmth fills me that has nothing to do with the pint-sized heater in a pink fuzzy jumpsuit.

I want to make a baby.

Starting as soon as possible.

Tonight seems like a good time.

"I need to go." I speak the words with an edge of desperation.

Both John and Diane look at me funny.

Keeping her eyes on me, Diane carefully lifts Alene from my chest. Snuggling her face near the baby's head, she asks, "Everything okay?"

I rub my chest. "Yeah, I need to get home."

Alene's eyebrow goes up. Only the one. She holds out her hand in my direction. Her fingers are balled together, making a little fist. No, she's not reaching for me. Baby Day is waiting for a fist bump.

"Can't leave you hanging, short stuff." I lightly tap her hand with my knuckles before standing. "And with that, I'm outta here."

Maybe there is something powerful, some primal secret that calls to us through the baby scent. All the time I've spent with Alene today has me racing to get home to Hailey. The urge to procreate engulfs me. I want to drag her to my cave and plant my seed in her.

What the fuck is going on?

I hold off jogging to my truck until the front door closes behind me. Barely.

CHAPTER 4

$\mathcal{A}$s soon as the door closes, I'm running to my truck and throwing it into gear.

Next thing I know, I'm speeding down the road to our house.

Getting here is a blur. I don't remember making any turns.

The car behind me flicks their high beams and my heart stalls thinking I'm about to be pulled over. Instead they pass me and I see it's Erik's Bronco. I flip him off and he gives me the same in his rearview window.

Smug bastard.

His Naked Whidbey bumper sticker makes me laugh, though. Talk about growing up and owning your shit.

Distracted by Erik, I almost miss my mailbox marking the private drive. Slamming on the breaks, I take the turn to quickly and squash a couple of ferns at the edge, but don't take out the post or the mailbox. I consider this a success.

Gravel spins out from my tires when I reach the house. Except for the porch light being on, the house is dark. A glance at the truck's clock tells me it's not even eight o'clock. Hailey can't possibly be in bed yet.

Where is she?

Her not being home is going to put the kibosh on my plans to have sex with her.

In a major way.

I scowl at the empty spot where her car should be, then text her.

GET HOME

NOW

I realize the all caps might come off as angry. Especially after our fight this morning. Not that I'm agreeing it was even a fight. More of a squabble, a minor dispute over three words.

Please I add.

Nameless barrels into me when I open the door, nearly knocking me off my feet. He might not be a year old yet, but he's the size of a horse. A pony at least. He puts his paws on my stomach while his tail thumps wildly around my legs.

"Someday we'll give you a proper name." I scratch his head. "Wanna go outside?"

At the sound of his favorite two words, he dashes past me into the yard and toward my truck. Sitting next to the front wheel, he looks at me expectantly.

"Sorry, buddy. We're not going anywhere."

He tilts his head and barks once.

"I don't know where she is, so we can't go find her."

It's probably my imagination, but I swear he gives me a dirty look right before he lifts his leg to pee on my tire.

Message received.

"Listen, you giant poodle, I can still build you a dog house over there." I point to my workshop on the far side of the clearing.

He shakes his collar and trots over to me as light breaches the tree line. Anticipating the arrival of his favorite human, he paces in front of me. "Down boy."

I could tell myself the same thing. I'm still sporting a semi after having dirty thoughts the entire drive home.

The silver hood of Hailey's SUV comes into view. Nameless

runs in circles, bouncing around like a fuzzy deer. Honestly, he's more cartoon than dog.

When she stops the engine and opens her door, Nameless leaps onto her lap. Not that there's room for him, but that doesn't stop him. He licks all over Hailey's face.

I want to be the one licking her.

Not necessarily her face.

Especially now that it's covered in dog spit.

I'm jealous and needy. It's making me cranky.

Neither Hailey nor I have said anything. Her expression tells me she's still a little mad from this morning. Over the dog's head, she stares at me, not smiling or looking happy to see me. At all.

I squint at her and cross my arms.

"Okay, that's enough, sweet boy. Let's go." Nameless finally jumps out of the vehicle and sits on the dirt, patiently waiting for her.

At least one of us is patient.

I don't want her to be mad at me anymore. Hell, I really don't want her to ever be mad at me. I'm always going to say and do stupid shit, but I've learned a thing or two over the past year.

I stalk toward her, keeping my eyes focused on hers. I pout my lips and lower my eyebrows to copy her face. Silently, I pull her out of her seat, then shove the door closed.

She parts her lips. "I—"

I silence her with my mouth.

Nothing she could say is more important than kissing her in this moment.

Nothing.

Instead of melting into me the way I love, she tenses. Her hands stay at her sides.

She is my world and I need to remind her. I need to claim her as mine.

I pull her close against me. My fingers tangle in her hair and I angle her head to kiss her deeper. Slowly her arms wrap around my waist.

Yes, Hailey. Forgive my stupid mouth from earlier. Let me make it right.

Her tongue sweeps over my bottom lip. With a relieved moan, I respond and take control of the kiss again.

Shifting us to be against the side of the SUV, I grind my hips against hers. I'm fully hard and needing her.

My breath is coming in short pants from our kissing. I move my mouth to her jaw, kissing a line from her lips to her ear. Using my nose, I nuzzle down her throat. My closed lips retrace the line. Open and wet kisses follow.

"Tom?" Hailey's voice sounds uncertain and a little confused.

"Shh," I whisper against her skin. "Let me apologize."

"You—" She swallows the rest of her words when I cup her breast through her shirt.

"Let me show you how much I love you." I rub my erection against her.

The contact seems to convince her I'm serious. Her fingers grip my hips, pulling me even closer to her.

Now I have her full attention.

With my hands on her ass, I lift her up. She wraps her legs around my hips, her heat presses against me. There is too much fabric separating me from her skin.

Part of her weight is braced on the SUV, so I'm able to hold her with one arm. I take advantage of this to sneak the other hand under her shirt. I find her nipple already hard and ready for me. I free it from her bra, pinching and rolling it between my fingers. I love the feel of her skin.

She palms me through my jeans and I nearly explode.

God, I want this woman. I need to be inside her.

Now.

We're alone. No one can see us unless they drive down our

private road. Who would randomly show up on a Saturday night? We don't know those kind of assholes.

I reach for the button of her jeans. "These need to come off."

In response, she loosens her grip on my hips and lets her legs slide to the ground. After she toes off her sneakers, her fingers fumble and shove the denim to the ground. Without embarrassment she stands in front of me, beautifully exposed below the waist.

I unzip my own fly. I really want her naked, but the urge to be inside her is stronger than my patience for removing more clothes than absolutely necessary. I'm almost blind with need for her right now.

Her hands reach inside my fly and pull my cock out. She gives it a not so gentle squeeze. I lean into her and bite her earlobe.

With my lips against her ear, "This is where I asked you to marry me. Right here. You said you would be mine forever."

I recapture her lips and take her mouth with my tongue. It's not gentle. There's nothing sweet about my need for her right now.

"I'm yours," she whispers.

I practically growl when I slide my fingers between her legs. She's as turned on right now as I am.

For a split second, the words I've been thinking for the past hour fill my throat. I want to tell her, but first I need to prove she's really mine.

I lift her again, placing her legs around my hips. She's still holding my cock and guides it to her opening.

I lower her over me. With one quick thrust, we're joined together.

Hailey folds her arms around my shoulders. Her thighs tighten when she crosses her ankles behind my back.

I'm momentarily lost in her. As relief settles inside me, I exhale and rest my head on her breast.

"Tom?"

I can't speak. Too many emotions flood my system. Relief, need, desire, fear… this need to possess her scares me.

I kiss the swell of her breast through her shirt before rolling my hips and pulling out slightly. Slowly I push back into her.

It's too much.

My base instincts kick in. On the next thrust, I pound into her.

God, she feels amazing. I do it again.

Her short nails dig into my shoulders and she holds on. That's about all she can do with me pinning her to the car and driving into her like a maniac.

"Sweetheart?" Her voice breaks through my lust.

I open my eyes in panic. "Did I hurt you?"

"No, but I think someone's coming." She points behind me.

Sure enough, headlights near the main road have swung in our direction.

"Who would be an asshole and randomly show up?" I tighten my grip on her ass. "Hold on tight."

She takes me literally and clenches around my cock, which is still buried in her.

I jog to the front door, bouncing her on me in the strangest, but good way. Nameless runs ahead of us.

"I've never had running sex before." Her words fade into giggles as she reaches into my back pocket, giving my ass a squeeze.

'No time for admiring my ass." I fumble up the steps as lights sweep over our parked cars. We're still in shadow when I get the door open and stumble us both through it, nearly tripping over the dog.

I turn the lock and lean Hailey against solid wood. Luckily the lights are off and we can't be seen from the windows.

She's still giggling. I cover her mouth with my hand to muffle her. She nips at my palm. I replace my hand with my lips. That works much better.

Remembering I'm still inside her, I thrust gently to remind her we're still joined.

Heavy footsteps echo on the porch a few feet away. The hairs on my neck stand up in defense.

Hailey and I both freeze. Leaning away from her enough to see her face, I notice her eyes are wide. I can't tell if she's afraid, surprised, or excited. Maybe all three.

Pounding sounds on the door behind her head.

I hold my breath. I'm pretty sure Hailey does the same. Nameless goes over to the window and barks.

"Shh." I hush him as quietly as possible.

"Tom? Hailey?" Kelso calls from the porch. "Are you guys in there? I found a pair of shoes and women's jeans by Hailey's car."

"Kelso," I mumble in disgust.

Hailey giggles softly. I press my lips against hers. Sassy girl sticks her tongue in my mouth and squeezes my cock. I'm still hard, but her actions are making me harder. It's torture not to move.

"Hello?" Erik pauses his knocking. Finally. "Hello?"

Not willing to deny myself from pleasure just because Kelso is the kind of asshole who can't buy a clue. I swing us away from the door and tap Hailey's thigh.

She gives me another squeeze, then stands up.

Reluctantly, I slide out of her.

Damn cockblocking Kelso. Ever since he was eyeing Hailey last year like a piece of his favorite chocolate cake, he's been on my list.

I flip off the door.

I'm half tempted to open it. Let him see what he's interrupting. Hailey being embarrassed is what stops my hand on the handle.

She taps my arm, drawing my focus back to her.

To answer the question in her eyes, I indicate the hallway and put my finger to my lips. We creep away from the door like a couple of teenagers sneaking home after curfew.

Unable to keep my hands to myself, I pinch her glorious ass as she climbs the stairs ahead of me.

Once safely upstairs, her giggles turn into full laughter. "How long do you think he's going to stand out there knocking on the door?"

"Knowing him, we'll find him out there in morning." That's a lie. I'm sure he'll give up soon. Probably.

"Aren't you curious what he wants?"

We're in our bedroom. Our bed is a few feet away. Kelso is the last thing on my mind right now. I prowl in Hailey's direction until her legs bump into the mattress. "Who?"

Her smile tells me she gets it. "Maybe it's an emergency?"

"Then he should call 911." I shove her jacket off her shoulders and start undoing her shirt buttons. Her bra falls to the floor.

She yanks my T-shirt up my torso. To help her, I pull it off by grabbing the back. I have to sit down to take off by boots. She kneels in front of me to help pull them off and quickly does the same with my jeans and boxers. Her fingers glide over the new scar on my leg before she softly kisses the raised skin.

We're naked.

Took long enough.

Her hand finds my cock again. Despite our interruption, I'm still mostly hard. My balls are a little blue. I wonder how that affects my swimmers.

I'll need to do some research.

The reason for attacking Hailey by her car comes back to me.

Baby making.

Or practicing.

I pull Hailey up at the same time I lie on the bed. Her hair tickles my chest when she leans forward and straddles me.

"Where were we?" Her soft kisses mark my skin.

I roll her off of me and slide between her legs. "Somewhere around here."

I kiss below her breasts. "Or maybe here?"

"I think you were lower." She strokes my hair.

"Was I?" I drag my nose along her hip. "This doesn't seem familiar."

"Lower." She lifts her hips and pushes my head farther south with her hands.

Adjusting myself against the sheets, I shift my body down the bed.

"Yes, that is beginning to feel familiar." She grins down at me.

I smile into the skin of her inner thigh before kissing the same spot.

The urge to claim her fades. Replacing it is the need to worship her body.

Soft licks and kisses make her squirm. Her fingers tighten to let me know she's had enough of my teasing. I chuckle and lift my head.

"Thomas, stop this nonsense and love me right."

"Ooh, full name. You don't scare me, Idaho. You know I always love you right." I narrow my eyes at her while I sweep my tongue over the spot that usually makes her moan. I'm rewarded with the response I'd hoped for.

"Cat got your tongue?" I gently suck on the same spot.

She fists the comforter. "Cat's got something."

I love this woman.

I hum against her and around her. She squirms in the best way.

Following her cues, I love her body, bringing her to the edge, then easing up.

I slide two fingers into her slick warmth, curling them to find *that* spot.

Her eyes flutter closed when I hit it.

A familiar trembling begins and I know she's close. This time I don't stop. I keep up the same pressure and pace, watching her beautiful face as she comes.

I kiss her hip, and she bucks off the bed.

Without pausing, I slip back inside her. Kissing her neck, her jaw, the corner of her mouth, I can't get enough of her. We're as close as two people can be, and it's still not enough.

I need more.

I need to expand this love inside me.

"Let's have a baby," I whisper against her lips.

CHAPTER 5

"*L*et's make a baby." I repeat watching as her eyes widen and her pupils dilate.

"Right now?" Her voice is nothing more than a whisper.

I slowly move inside her. "Sure."

"Oh…" Her breath catches.

"Breathe, Hailey." I stroke down her cheek with the back of a finger. Tracing her jaw, I trail that finger down her neck, over her collarbone and down the center of her chest.

Her chest trembles with her inhale.

"Um, I'm on the pill. Remember?" She doesn't blink, her eyes searching mine.

Of course. I honestly forgot. I still my movements, but don't withdraw.

"Maybe you should stop." Leaning forward, I kiss the spot near her ear that always makes her moan.

"Having sex with you? Or taking the pill?"

I cup her breast and squeeze. "Definitely not the sex part.

I roll us so she's on top of me, her knees straddling my hips. I weave my fingers through hers and lift her hands to my mouth, slowly kissing my way across each of her knuckles.

She sighs. "Are you sure?"

Afraid to say something stupid, I nod, looking into her eyes.

"Oh…"

I kiss her palm before placing it over my heart. I move our other hands, fingers still woven together, and rest them on her lower stomach, below her belly button. I nod again. "Never been so sure about something that scares me so much."

My focus is on our hands over her belly as I lose myself in thoughts of feeling and watching it swell with a baby we'll make together.

Her fingers spread over my heart. "Tom?"

I lift my gaze from her stomach to her face.

"Are you serious?"

"What makes you think I'm joking about this?" I gently press against her hand, then let my hand skim her skin down to where she ends and I begin.

She shifts above me, gently tipping her hips. I'm reminded of our connection. It's not only sexual. I'm hers, all of me. Heart, soul, and body.

"I want to make babies with you. I want little versions of us running around in the world. Dimples, long legs, beautiful, kind, stubborn humans that are half you and half me."

She pinches my nipple. "The stubborn and dimple parts they'll get from you, right?"

I flinch, but grin. Holding her hips, I pull her down further onto me. "Say yes."

Tears sparkle in her eyes. "I already said yes when you proposed last year."

"Let's set a date. Let's make babies."

Her laughter tickles my skin when she leans forward. "Which one do you want to do first?"

"Does it matter?"

"How about we start with the wedding and one baby?"

I frown and press my lips together. "Okay on the wedding, if it's soon. By the end of the year. I want you knocked up and barefoot by Christmas."

"That's so romantic."

"Fine. You can wear socks. I know how you hate cold feet."

A small smile tugs at her lips.

"Since you get the socks, how do you feel about twins? Go for the twofer?"

Her eyes widen again and she stills her slow grind. We're talking more than we're having sex right now despite me being completely buried inside her and her naked boobs inches from my mouth.

"Think how great twin boys would be?" I tease her breast, bringing it close to my lips so I can gently bite her nipple. She doesn't move or speak. With my mouth still on her, I study her face above me. I use my teeth to get her attention.

"Twin boys? *Two* Donnely boys?" Her stare is faraway. I can't tell if the idea delights or terrifies her.

I kiss her nipple and release her. "Or girls. Or one of each. You know, triplets."

It's an old joke, but it makes her laugh.

"Us as parents." Her voice falters.

"We're going to be amazing. Much better than John. I found Alene in the dog crate today."

"Again?"

We both chuckle.

Our eyes meet and our smiles mirror each other. I lean up on my elbows to reach her mouth. She meets me halfway, slipping her tongue between my lips. The need for words disappears as our bodies move together. I tangle my fingers into her hair, gently tugging her head back to look into her eyes. Our breaths mix together when I use my hands on her hips to increase our rhythm.

I circle my thumb in the spot that drives her wild. She arches her back and comes apart above me as another orgasm hits her. This is the kind of two-fer she loves.

My thrusts stall and become erratic as her pulsing pushes me into my own orgasm.

We won't make a baby tonight.

I'll try to be patient. I'm not promising I'll be successful.

I drift off to sleep thinking about fat babies with dimples and dark hair.

OLAF'S CHRISTMAS CAROL

A CROSSOVER CHRISTMAS SHORT

INTRODUCTION

Originally shared exclusively with my newsletter subscribers.

My 2016 holiday short starring everyone's favorite Whidbey bartender, Olaf. I love writing these future glimpses into the characters' lives at the holidays.

Look for a new holiday novella coming out late 2017.

A VERY MERRY OLAF CHRISTMAS

"*I*t's the hap, happiest time—"

No.

No more.

The carolers have surrounded my front door again and are caterwauling loud enough to send the town's feline population into spontaneous heat. If I had a fire hose, I'd spray them silent. The town should give me a medal for restoring peace and quiet.

Enough!

A man can only handle a certain amount of cheer before his brain begins to seep out his ears and his soul shrivels into a dried husk in the hollow shell of his chest.

No, not a roasted chestnut shell either.

Don't get me started on all the traditional garbage women force their families to eat because it's Christmas.

Fruitcake is a monstrous abomination of the words fruit and cake.

Mincemeat? In a pie? Stop it right now. No, I don't care if nuts and raisins are involved. You lost me at the word mincemeat. Not to mention raisins.

I had a grandmother who liked to set a plum pudding on fire

after she dramatically turned off all the lights in the dining room on Christmas Eve. In my innocence, I was fascinated by lighting food on fire. That had to mean it would be amazing. Wrong. I never expected her to make us eat the flaming corpse of my shattered Christmas illusions.

Another painful right of passage from childhood is discovering your parents made you sit on a strange man's lap and took pictures for posterity.

Is there something about the Santa suit that smells like urine or do they only hire incontinent men for the part? I'm asking for a friend. It's been years since I've been close enough to smell the foul stench of lies and stale beer.

To make the worst month of the year worse, I have to deal with the annual Sip n' Stroll taking over downtown Langley and clogging up the Dog House with merry revelers aka sippers who nurse a single beer and take up limited space for way too long.

Worse, the college kids, who are junior alcoholics, return to the island and think the law of the great state of Washington doesn't apply to them or their half-pickled livers.

Hiring a bouncer to sit at the door and check IDs costs me money.

"Bah humbug," I mutter to myself as I pull a pitcher for a group of grown ups wearing green-striped onesie pajamas and Santa hats.

I hope the good baby Jesus can't see the festival of the ridiculous his birthday has become.

"Olaf, did you just say—" John Day asks from the other side of the counter where he's waiting for his own pitcher. Thank the sweet Baby Jesus he's wearing normal pants. His dark eyes hold a concern I've finally cracked my nut.

"Bah humbug." I spit out the words, carefully enunciating my disdain. "And don't go calling me Scrooge. Ebenezer was a rich man. You see any bags of gold sitting around this place?"

"I think you're confusing the Dickens character with Scrooge

McDuck, Old Man." Tom Donnely shares his unwanted opinion from the other side of John. I didn't see him come in. He's sporting one of those neon orange Carhatt beanies over his shaggy blond hair. The man always needs to be the center of attention. Guess dressing like a traffic cone works.

"You call me old again and you're banned for the rest of the year."

"That's only ten days. Might be worth it." The light to John's dark, Donnely strokes his blond beard in thought. "You going to have your tough bouncer throw me out, too?"

I follow the jerk of his head to the man outside the door. Carter Kelso, wearing a set of reindeer antlers, is set up on a stool outside. He brought his own flashlight to check for fake IDs. I have little faith in either Kelso off-spring, but he eagerly volunteered for a few pitchers of beer and an agreement I'll recommend his goat business.

The boy is starting a goat business. I have no words for that nonsense.

At least it's better than last year when his younger brother stole one of my stools to take advantage of the mistletoe vandals hang all over town every year. Okay, the vandals are really the Ladies of Perpetual Annoyance or some other committee formed to better the town and bug honest business owners like myself. Bunch of miscreants with access to a suspicious amount of ribbon, if you ask me.

"Shouldn't you be home with your women instead of harassing me in my own establishment?"

John shrugs. "Diane's with Hailey down the street buying yarn or something. They keep talking about learning how to crochet."

"Knit," Tom interjects and gives his friend a smug smirk. "Something about tiny booties for the next baby."

"Or your baby." John teases back.

Tom stills his face and flattens his lips. "I expect I'll know that information before you."

"Don't tell me if you're working on making that happen. Try to keep it to yourself," I say.

Tom gives me a small salute. "Speaking of our better halves, they may be awhile. I saw them go into the tasting room before we came in here. "

"With the baby?" I ask.

John smiles. "Alene doesn't mind. She loves the lights. And being snuggled against Diane is her favorite place to be."

"Can't blame her." Tom dodges John's attempt to slap his shoulder. "I'm talking about the warm comfort of a mother's touch. Jeez."

No way in hell his original comment is innocent.

Ignoring Tom, John continues talking with a soft look in his eyes like he wants to walk to the end of the block and check on his women. "My aunt will pick her up and bring her home for the night."

Tom's open palm successfully makes contact with his friend's shoulder. "Getting some action at the Saratoga tonight?"

"Aren't you banned from there?" I ask, already knowing the answer. During a holiday party for Donnely boats last week, Tom and Hailey got caught having relations in one of the inn's rooms. What a man and woman do behind closed doors is nobody's business. Unless the door and the room don't belong to them. Tom tried to blame it on being newlyweds, but management didn't buy it.

The couple from Indiana who had reserved the room wrote a helluva review on Trip Advisor. Heard Tom's already framed a copy.

"O!" a familiar voice shouts from the double-saloon doors. Erik Kelso shoves his way through the crowd.

"The night gets better," I mumble and start a pint for him.

I blink twice when he sets his hoof on the counter.

"What the hell is wrong with you?" I eye the rest of his get up. I expect Tom Donnely to be a ham, but after all that bullshit earlier this year with Erik's naked tuckus, you'd think he'd keep a low profile.

Not dress himself up as the Christmas ass.

Erik glances over his shoulder and then down at his brown furry chest. "Nothing?"

With a shake of my head, I point out the obvious. "You're a grown man. Halloween was two months ago."

John and Tom chuckle into their pint glasses.

"Where's the Christmas spirit, O? No respect for Rudolf?"

The red dot on his nose makes more sense now.

"The sign says no shirt, no service. Don't make me amend that to ban hooves in here. Again."

John coughs as he sputters on his beer. "Again?"

"Someone put a cow in the backroom in the early twentieth century when this was a private club. You boys should learn your island history better."

"When are you going to stop calling us boys?" Tom asks, looking put out.

"Never. You'll always be younger than me and lacking good sense. You paying for those beers? Or you want a tab?"

"Start a tab," Erik says. "On me."

My eyes bugs out a little at his offer. I've never known a Kelso to be generous when it comes to money. I knew they'd help out a friend without hesitation. Coffee business must be good.

"Oh for crying out loud," I say when I see Erik's wearing a fluffy deer tail on the back of his brown velvet costume. He catches me staring and shakes his backside for my benefit.

"The only onesie a grown man should wear is a Union Suit."

"With the trap door? Sexy, O!" Erik joins John and Tom at a table on the far side of the pool table.

I think about padding his bar tab for being a pain in my ass.

More people pile through the front door and fill the space around the stools. I'm grateful for hiring some kid as a bar back to help out during the holidays.

He's stranger than the Kelsos and named Falcon. Yes, that's really his name. I had to check his ID when I hired him.

And if he asks one more time if he can set up his drums in the corner for a drumming circle, I'm going to fire him.

Speaking of, where is that weirdo? We're running low on glasses. I scan the crowded room and spot his dreadlocked head next to Ashley Kingston's red curls.

For being smart enough to run a successful business, that girl has terrible taste in men.

I know her family and she's the perfect example of strict parenting inciting rebellion. For both her and her brother Jonah. He's got more holes in his head than God intended and she's got herself a bad reputation.

I'm about to throw something at Falcon's head to get his attention when Carter strides over and breaks up their conversation by stepping between the couple and turning his back on Falcon.

I can't hear Ashley's words, but from her tight expression I'm guessing she's not pleased.

This place has more drama than a soap opera. And I have a front row seat.

Lucky me.

Hold on. If Carter is pissing off Ashley, who's watching my door?

A monkey would do a better job at being a bouncer.

Falcon sets a tray of steaming hot glasses on the back bar with too much force, rattling the glass.

Perfect timing.

I put my hand on his shoulder like I'm offering him a promotion. "Get those organized and then go take over the door."

"Really?" His eyes light up.

I don't understand how this kid ticks. "Sure. Put on a jacket. It's cold out there."

"I never get cold." He bounces on his tip-toes and speeds off outside in his T-shirt and ripped jeans.

If he catches pneumonia, I'm going to put an ad out for a real trained monkey.

Dan keeps telling me I need to get more help in here and slow down.

At least he doesn't call me old to my face.

A breeze of fresh, but cold air blows through the open door. I see Falcon holding it open like a doorman. The thought he doesn't know what a bouncer does concerns me until I see a few familiar faces.

Maggie Marion and her group of friends stand near the door. I'm not too proud to admit I loved her mother, Ann, from afar for years before her death. She won me over with her baked goods and class despite being older than me by more than a decade. I think a lot of men around here had crushes on her. Her daughter sold the bakery, but carries the same sparkle as Ann did. Maggie's fella stands beside her along with another couple. A man holding a toddler is stuck between the swinging doors and the outside door.

I'm about to tell them this isn't a day care, when Diane walks in behind him carrying Alene.

The group of seven squeezes into an opening at the corner of the bar near the window. The little girl happily takes up residence on the bench in the window, patting the glass and smiling at the people outside.

Diane waves me over using Alene's chubby arm instead of her own hand.

"Kind of a late night for our little angel." My voice softens at the sight of Alene sitting on her mom's hip. Normally, kids aren't allowed in here in the evenings, but I guess I'll make an exception for this sweetheart. At least she's not trying to charm her way past Falcon. Yet.

"She's started fussing." Diane gives me a weak smile while bouncing Alene. "We're waiting on Helen to meet us here."

"Let me hold her." I extend my arms for Alene. She claps her mittened hands together and reaches for me.

"She's kind of going through a stranger-danger phase right now." Diane apologizes, but hands the pink bundle over the bar to me.

Alene attempts to tug my beard, but her fingers are trapped. Her forehead scrunches and her face darkens as she works herself up to a wail. I remove her mittens and set the world right.

Delighted, she tugs at my white whiskers.

"She probably thinks your the real Santa," Diane says softly. "You'd make the perfect one."

I stare into Alene's happy face.

Dammit if that little girl doesn't have us all wrapped around her fingers. Anything bad ever happens to her and it'd break all our hearts.

Yes, I have a heart. No, it's not three-sizes too small.

There's not a snowflake's chance in Phonenix I'm ever dressing up as Old Saint Nick.

"It's a Christmas miracle." Diane points to a quiet Alene, happily playing with my beard.

"Hello, Papa Silver Fox." The blond man with the toddler greets me with a friendly smile.

I lift an eyebrow at him.

"Quinn," Diane chides him. "Be nice to Olaf."

"I'm paying him a compliment! Silver foxes are all the rage. Hi, I'm Quinn." He extends his hand over the bar. I shift Alene and shake it. "The little one is Lizzy and the handsome man pretending to be a puppy with her is my husband, Ryan."

He says all of this as if I'll remember. "Nice to meet you."

The man and child in the window both give me friendly woofs.

Diane introduces me to the rest of her friends. I pretend I'm interested while smiling down at Alene.

"You should bring them to Sal's, Maggie." Diane gives her

former landlord a knowing smile. The kind of looks women exchange that send a nervous tremor down the spines of men.

"We went there for lunch. Unfortunately the resident silver fox is on vacation this week," Maggie answers.

"Selah was heartbroken," Maggie's guy Gil says.

A shorter woman with dark hair pokes her head around his tall frame. "You know what helps with heartbreak? Beer. What do you have that's extra hoppy. Cause it's the hop, hoppiest time of the year."

After singing the last sentence, she grins at me as if she somehow knows how much I hate that song. I sense a kindred sister of sarcasm.

Reluctantly returning Alene to her mother, I recommend an IPA and fill the rest of their order. The tall blond one named Kai, who looks like an old Viking, slides a fancy black credit card on the bar, subtly letting me know he's paying for whatever they drink. I appreciate a man who doesn't waffle when it comes to taking care of the check.

John wraps his thick arms around both Diane and Alene before kissing their cheeks. "Helen's outside in the car."

Diane's smiles and then frowns. "You think she'll be okay? It's her first overnight without us."

He kisses his wife softly on the lips and tells her, "Without us? Or us without her? We can cancel. Or go home early."

She frowns again. "And give up the chance at a full night's sleep? Are you crazy?"

He grumbles about priorities before she kisses his cheek. "I'll walk her out and be right back."

John watches them go with love in his eyes and all over his face like he got smashed with a love pie right in the kisser.

I remember that feeling. Best one in the world.

Before the divorce. Before the kids grew up and moved away.

When I was a young man in the Navy, I fell in love with a teacher from Oak Harbor. She wasn't charmed by my stories from around the world or my good looks. To a young buck with an ego, I accepted her challenge, making it my mission to make her fall in love with me. I sent her pearls from Japan and fancy perfume from France. Before I got transferred from Everett, I made her a promise. If she married me, as soon as I finished in the Navy, we'd move back to the island and never leave again.

I kept my end of the promise.

She now lives on a golf course in Phoenix with a retired insole salesman. Our youngest son, Neil, calls him Dad, too. Neil's always been a little prick. Steve at least remembers to call me on my birthday.

I'm the one who never left. Born here, I'm going to die here. Not for a long time, God willing.

Here's the part of the story where the ghosts of Christmas past, present, and future show up, isn't it?

"Bah humbug," I grumble under my breath.

"Did you just say—" Diane asks as she returns childless.

"He's been muttering it all night." John slings an arm over her shoulder. "Shall we go take advantage of our hotel room?"

She grins and nods. "I made sure to avoid the Room of Unmentionable Things."

"I heard that! I highlighted that quote in the review!" Holding up his arm in triumph, Tom shouts from his table. How he heard her from across the room, I can't figure out. I can barely hear myself complain in my own head. Hailey nudges his shoulder and lowers his arm.

I watch John and his wife say good-bye to their friends, and dammit if my heart doesn't feel fuzzy and warm.

One thing people either get or don't get about this island is we're all family. We have a bunch of crazy aunts in those ribbon-wielding gossipers, Sandy, Connie, and Sally. They meddle and gossip because they care. The brotherhood of friends with John and Tom at the heart is as strong as blood. No longer boys, they've become honorable men. For the most part. Maggie's circle is the only family she has now that her parents have passed. Knowing she is loved and cared for would make Ann happy again. As the younger generation pairs off and starts their own broods, our family grows and expands to include the newcomers like Dan, his lady Roslyn, sweet Diane, and even the younger Kelso's girl, Cari. Despite our differences, Dan's become a true friend to me, pushing back the loneliness solitary life can bring. Our family happily welcomes home the wayward sons and daughters like Hailey King. Hell, I'd greet my own boys with open arms and a smile if they came to visit.

Some may say we're stuck in the past here. Those people are the ones who don't understand the magic of life in a small town.

I feel a lump lodge in my throat and a burning behind my eyes.

Dammit.

"Bah humbug," I grumble to dispel the feelings filling up my crotchety old heart.

"Merry Christmas to you, too!" Tom shouts from the corner.

The Kelsos follow his lead and raise their voices. "Merry Christmas to us all."

Next thing I know, the whole crowd is echoing their words with glee.

"Merry Christmas, one and all," I softly say, catching Maggie's eye.

Louder, I shout. "Merry Christmas to all. Now go home. It's last call."

THE PINK PEARL

A PIROTICA SHORT

INTRODUCTION

First published under Selah Elmore's pen name, *The Pink Pearl* was the name of one of Selah's erotica books in *Geoducks Are for Lovers*. I had a blast writing a pirate story and always promised myself I'd write more. Someday. Maybe.

This short is different than the rest. For one thing, there are sword jokes and pirate puns.

If you've been reading my books since the beginning in 2013, you might remember this tale of sexy pirates on the high seas.

Published under the pen name Suzette Marquis

Suzette Marquis is the pen name of Selah Elmore, who is a fictional character created by Daisy Prescott. Still with me? Suzette writes steamy tales of pirates when not daydreaming about lumberjacks and bearskin rugs. Daisy Prescott is a full time writer, who dreams up characters who demand their own publications.

CHAPTER 1

Fiona

Sweat began to drip down her chest, pooling between her breasts. She noticed his hair along his brow was dampened from his own exertion.

Fair Robert thrust as she retreated. Sprung free from the leather strip that normally bound them, his long golden locks hung in his face

He pulled back before thrusting again. She mirrored his actions. When he advanced, Fiona responded, her muscles clenching as she reacted to him.

With one final thrust, she came undone. Literally. The tip of his sword untied her chemise, freeing her full breasts to the cool, morning sea air.

"Had enough, Mistress Fiona?" he asked.

"You do not play fair, Robert. Hardly more than a glancing blow, certainly not deadly." She glanced down at her perked nipples. "Not even un petit mort."

His answering smirk was meant to disarm her, but she wasn't finished with their sparring. As he stared at her exposed chest, she swiftly sliced the air with her own sword, flicking his unguarded blade down toward the floor of the cabin. Her own sharp edge tore through the laces of his breeches before settling its point at the newly exposed skin.

"Your cockiness always gets you into trouble." She smiled, watching as the cream colored linen slid down his hips, exposing the skin of his hipbones and a noticeable trail of hair.

"I do believe it is my cockiness that attracted you first, mi'lady."

"No. It was the sight of your ass bent over the rigging that first caught my eye. Luckily for me, your face lived up to your name."

A swift movement, a parry, and his blade clanked against hers once again. Ignoring that her breasts were exposed, she advanced on him, forcing him into the corner of the cabin.

"Shall I threaten you with the plank?"

"You can threaten me all you would like. However, I'll never walk the plank and we both know it," he said, his voice husky from their sparring.

"I know nothing of the kind. You disobey me, you'll get the plank. Or marooned. My ship, my rules. You are aboard the ship at my pleasure. Displease me, and you'll be cast adrift without your sword." Gliding the weapon over her head and then down, she deflected his blade. "Double cross me, and the family jewels will stay with me."

"I shall assume, by your scowl, double cross is not the double the lady prefers."

"You assume correct. And I prefer your sword still attached."

His haughty laughter filled the cabin. "Without my sword, what would be left of me?"

"Enough to feed the sharks. Let them fight over the scraps." She moved to deflect his advance and found herself with her back against the post of her bed.

"Ah, my mistress finds herself with nowhere to escape." He leered.

His bare chest heaved with his breath as she let her eyes drift lower. And lower still, wondering how his breeches stayed on him. When her eyes reached the apex of his thighs, she found her answer.

Taking advantage of his overconfidence, she allowed him to step closer. Sensing he was leaning in for a kiss, rather than a final blow, she wrapped her calf around his leg. This threw him off balance and he stumbled back as his breeches slipped lower on his hips. His erection sprang free when he landed on the silk, Oriental rug covering the wood floor.

"Well, well. I seem to have full advantage now." She licked her lips and watched him bob free. After flicking her gaze over her shoulder at the large mahogany captain's bed, she quickly glanced back at him.

"I can tell from the flush in your cheeks and your pert nipples that you like what you see. Perhaps I shall avoid another day being a meal for the sharks."

"Perhaps. Although, I'm not sure I'm done playing with you. I'm thinking of the strap or maybe my whip since you prove no challenge with your blade. Now that our clothes are in tatters, are you going to keep me waiting longer?"

"Let me state that although I enjoy the sting of your whip, I believe earlier you mentioned un petite mort. Shall we change the game?"

Her eyes traveled from the juncture of his legs, following that trail of hair up and over his stomach to his chest. Each group of muscles formed its own continent in the topography of his abdomen. Shadows and ridges outlined his pure masculine form. Briefly meeting his eyes, she shrugged what remained of her chemise from her shoulders, leaving her bare in the early light of morning peeking through the portholes of her cabin.

With a swift movement, she was on her back on the bed, Fair Robert leaning over her.

"Where was I?" he asked, a devilish gleam in his eyes.

"Much further south, I believe." She shoved his head below her equator. "And practicing your French."

"Oui," he murmured against her inner thigh. It was the last words uttered in either French or English for several moments.

The scruff of his cheek dragged along her thigh while his hands splayed her open for his mouth. Whether he was practicing his French or Latin, he showed great enthusiasm for his task. Each swirl of his tongue, pressure from his lips, and movement of his fingers inside her brought her closer to her release.

As the promised orgasm tightened her muscles, Fiona clawed at his long, golden locks. Her legs tightened around his neck and shoulders, and she swore he must be able to breathe through his ears.

After her spasms ceased, her legs turning from steel to jelly, she lifted her head to catch him staring at her with a self-satisfied grin.

"Did I please you, mi'lady?"

"You always do. It's why I keep you around rather than toss you into the sea with the morning's chamber pots."

"You must admit, you'd miss me if I wasn't here."

"I'd miss your tongue and your cock. However, both can be replaced. I have an entire crew who possess one of each, except those who have been gelded." She paused, watching the grimace cross his face. "When we go ashore today in Port de Neuf, I am certain I will find more able bodied and willing seamen to satisfy my needs."

"Ouch. Mistress, you wound my heart with your words."

"Your ego seems to be in fine shape." She took his sizable, rigid length in her hand. "Now, I think I'm ready for a different kind of sword play."

Fair Robert

The *Mi'Lady* docked a fair distance from the port-of-call. Gulls circled overhead and the sun shone down on the white sails of the ship as she anchored beyond the harbor barrier. The Jolly Roger flag had been taken down and replaced with the Union Jack while Captain Fiona Lindsley scowled. She planned to stay aboard the ship after commanding Fair Robert to take a small group ashore to collect supplies and procure the latest gossip. Robert knew that the last time in Port de Neuf had ended with a hasty retreat after Fiona was stopped and questioned on the dock by members of the British Royal Navy. She wasn't willing to risk such a meeting again so soon after the near miss last month. The last thing they needed was to encounter a flotilla of war ships with eager seamen searching for the Pink Pearl. Or making enquiries about the captain of the *Mi'Lady*.

Ashore, Robert left Sebastien and One Eyed Jack to gather supplies. He excused himself, saying he had a special, private errand for the captain. After making his way up the hill of the small port town with its brightly painted buildings to the Golden

Parrot tavern, he entered a narrow, cobblestone alley. Glancing around to ensure he wasn't followed, he saw only the tavern's strapping, young cook, who was occupied tossing gray water into the gutter when he entered through the back door.

He purposely sat at a small wood table in the corner of the tavern, too far from the weak light of the front door and the bar to be noticed by the small cluster of patrons. The tavern was quiet and the few drunks at the bar would be poor witnesses should things go afoul. He smiled at his cleverness and took a drink of his beer. With his back to the wall, he waited, digging his nail into the soft wood of the scarred and stained table top. Dressed in a flowing white shirt, pale tan trousers, and his typical faded brocade vest, he had attempted to appear discreet. He had even pulled his hair into a tidy ponytail at the nape of his neck.

His pint of ale and his patience were almost finished when a man in the uniform of the British Navy entered the tavern and stood near the bar. He was paunchy and his hair was thinning, despite looking no older than Robert's twenty-five years. Perhaps he was a well-fed officer. With a small nod from Robert, the man joined him at the table in the corner.

"You have information about a rare pearl?" the sailor asked, giving Robert the once over.

"I might. Did you bring what was promised?" he responded.

"Aye," the man said. Reaching into his pocket, he produced a small, brown leather pouch, bulging and heavy in appearance.

Robert took the bag and weighed it in his hand before tossing it once.

"What information are you seeking?" Robert asked, tucking the pouch safely inside his vest. He knew better than to ask any names. In these transactions, names were unnecessary and dangerous. "The pearl you seek is no ordinary gem. It is far more priceless than the rarest diamond from Africa, and more coveted than all the rum on the islands. A small bag of coins will only buy a few clues."

"You are confident in your position, Robert. Or shall I call you Fair Robert?" At his surprised expression, the stranger continued, "Oh, I've done my research. I know quite a bit about you. Orphaned, and raised in a brothel, you're a buccaneer, and dare I say, scoundrel. You've earned the reputation of a rapscallion across the seas."

"Your knowledge is impressive, but mine is what you seek. I believe that gives me an advantage. This," he said, gesturing to the pouch tucked safely inside his vest, "is a promise that you will receive some of what you seek today, and the rest upon delivery of the gem."

"Fair point. If we attain the pearl, you will be rich beyond your imagination. As we agreed."

"The pearl is closer than you believe. You are looking in the wrong area."

"We've searched the coast and waters all around Jamaica last month. There was no sign, no hint or evidence, of any pearl. Not even idle gossip from drunken lips."

"Perhaps what you seek is not what you've been told."

"Rear Admiral Lindsley has been reticent to give details other than this pink pearl must be found and returned to him."

"Are you familiar with corsairs, sir? I would imagine that a man such as you, with all the ribbons and epaulettes of your ranking, would be."

"If you are referring to those despicable pirates, of course. Calling them corsairs or buccaneers only romanticizes their wicked ways."

"That is your first clue, sir."

"The pearl is being held by pirates? As booty? As ransom?"

"Hardly, but you are warmer."

The stranger furrowed his brow. Robert waited, sipping his ale. It wasn't for him to solve the mystery. His goal with this game of cat and mouse was to make himself a wealthy man.

"Are you suggesting that what the Rear Admiral seeks is not a gem at all?"

"I am. Nevertheless, the value of the Pink Pearl is a price far above rubies."

"You speak in riddles, Fair Robert. I have not given you a ransom of pieces of eight only to be told tall tales."

"To summarize what I've told you so far, since you insist on being a block of wood, the pearl you seek is not a gem. Nor is it to be found on land. Ask yourself what the admiral treasures above all things and you will have your answer."

A silence lingered over the table.

"I believe you are a liar as well as a scoundrel. Dare you infer that the admiral is seeking not a gem, but his niece Fiona? The beloved daughter of his only sister who was lost to sea while returning to school in England from Jamaica over ten years ago?"

"I do, and I am. Long has there been rumors of a fair pirate on these seas. One whose beauty is matched by her ruthlessness and sexual prowess. This may be the gem your admiral has you hunting."

"Blasphemy! That maiden went down with the ship. The tragedy killed her parents as well as devastated her uncle. He never recovered from their loss."

"Believe what you will, but should you discover you agree with my words, meet me back at this tavern in a month's time. Bring a larger pouch and I may be able to be of further assistance."

Robert drained the dregs of the amber liquid from his tankard and stood. He nodded to his companion, but made no move to leave first. He suspected he'd be followed the moment his boot crossed the threshold.

"One month's time. I'll hold you to it or be seeing you on the scaffolds." The sailor stood, donned his hat, and with a nod, departed through the door he entered the tavern.

Robert patted his vest and walked into the kitchen. After looking down both directions of the alley, he walked toward the busier street and down the hill in the direction of the awaiting skiff and crew.

Drunken laughter, barrels being hauled aboard ships, and the sound slapping of water against wood greeted him as he turned the corner onto the quay, but the noise of a scuffle behind him distracted him. Turning and drawing his knife, he discovered Sebastien standing over the body of a man in dark clothing.

"Do you know this man?" Sebastien asked. "He's been trailing you since the tavern." He kicked the unconscious man in the back with his rough boot.

Upon closer inspection, Robert recognized him as the cook from the tavern. "Aye, he is the cook at that rat infested tavern. I knew I'd be followed. Let's bring him back with us. He can be the captain's new pet."

With a whistle, Sebastien called over Jack. The two of them lifted the cook and dragged him to their skiff hidden between the larger ships at the main pier.

CHAPTER 3

Fiona

The rocking of the ship while she sailed away from Port de Neuf and the danger of the British Royal Navy soothed Fiona as she gazed down at the handsome face of the man in her bed. The man from the docks was lying across her bed, stripped from the waist up, and if it weren't for the shackles around his wrists and ankles, he could be her lover. *Even shackled, he could be my lover*, she thought and smiled.

The beating of the waves against the hull created a rhythm that echoed her heartbeat. A warm, tropical breeze blew in through the portholes of her cabin and reminded her there was no place she'd rather be than at sea on her beloved ship. Any sort of bounty or treasure was secured below deck or hidden in one of the many caves in secluded coves known only to a trusted few. Looking around the cabin, her eyes landed on the few trinkets and treasures she kept for sentimental reasons. A silver candelabrum, a strand of pearls, and a silver hand mirror with broken glass were scattered across the marble of her dresser. Another candelabrum, brass spyglass, and nautical charts littered her desk. At night, crystal-hung candle sconces bathed the cabin in a soft light, but last night's candles had burned out hours ago.

The man looked peaceful as he slept. At least she thought he was asleep. The bump on his head from Sebastian last night was bruised and swollen.

Fiona reached out to stroke his dark locks where they fell across his face. His profile reminded her of an English illustration from her childhood books. Images of rosy cheeked boys marching in their uniforms flitted through her memory, and she struggled to squelch the longing they stirred within her for a life lost fathoms deep in the unforgiving waters of the Atlantic a very long time ago.

Her guest's moans brought her back to the present and she quickly removed her hand from his forehead before she was caught being affectionate to him. The Captain of the *Mi'Lady* was never affectionate. With anyone.

Another moan and the man struggled to lift his hand from the bed only to be met with the resistance from his ropes.

She stared at his face, willing him to open his eyes so she could delve into the mystery of his appearance on her ship. After a few moments of aggravated waiting, she flicked his pectoral with the cat o'nine tails before returning it to her lap.

As his skin began to pink where the leather strips made impact, the man opened his eyes.

"It would appear the Adonis has deemed this mere human worthy of his attention. Finally," she said, flicking the braided leather tendrils lightly against her own leg.

"Forgive me for keeping you waiting, mistress ..." He faded into silence.

"You may call me Captain. You find yourself aboard my ship, Mister ..." Her own words left room for him to answer. She doubted if his name would be his own.

"Boarder. William Boarder, Captain."

"Ah, Mr. Boarder. The pleasure is all mine." Her gaze moved

from his deep brown eyes, over his strong jaw, before lingering on his skin just above his unlaced, but still closed, breeches.

"I doubt that with every breath I take."

She smiled. "Have you just declared that every breath belongs to me? A very bold, and perhaps foolish, declaration. Which are you, William Boarder? Bold or foolish?

"A bit of both, I believe, Captain." He tugged at his bonds, demonstrating he was completely under her control. "For I seem to already be at your mercy."

"I'm not known for my mercy. It is the least of my traits." To emphasize this, she flicked his chest again with the flogger, only this time she left a welt. "Tell me this, Mr. Boarder, how did you come to be in this situation? I am most curious."

He blanched and then blinked a few times before composing his answer. "I'm not exactly certain how I came to discover myself here. I'm uncertain as to where here is other than in the captain's quarters of a ship that is at sea. My last memory is of being on the quay of Port de Neuf. Forgive me if the rest is a blank, but from the ache in my head, I suspect I bear the mark of one of your men upon my skull." He squinted his eyes as if in pain.

"Aye, you do indeed. My crew does not take lightly to being followed and spied upon. Spies are a dangerous lot. More foolish than bold."

"My apologies, mistress. I will not insult your intelligence with lies. Tis true that I left the tavern to follow your man to the quay. I was concerned with his safety after his meeting. There are ears and eyes of far less honorable men in both the tavern and darkened alleys. I was not aware he was traveling with companions. Overhearing a bit of his conversation led me to believe he would be in danger."

She remained silent for a moment, trying to sift the lies from the truth of his words. He followed Fair Robert that she knew was true, but upon what motivation? Robert was not a meek man who would appear to need protection. However, it appeared he did need to be watched. Fiona was unaware he met with anyone alone in Port de Neuf.

"Very strange of you to feel protective of a man such as the one you saw in the tavern. Perhaps you overheard something that piqued your curiosity?"

He gazed sheepishly into her eyes before answering. "Aye, mi' lady. I heard mentioned something about the legendary Pink Pearl. I'm only a lowly tavern cook. The promise of riches lured me to leave my senses and I acted foolishly."

Fiona swallowed her shock and quelled her rising emotions, lest her face gave anything away.

"The Pink Pearl? Bullocks. That is pure legend. And you thought you would follow my man and discover what men far more bold and stupid than a tavern cook have sought and failed to find for many a year? You, a landlubber who has probably never ventured further a sea than the harbor wall? Oh, dear. I had such high hopes for you. Pity."

His panicked eyes gave away his inner turmoil. He stretched his bindings, as if he could escape or break from his trussings. Her melodious laughter filled the room.

"Oh, sweet William. You cannot escape. As I see it, we have only two options. In most situations such as this there would only be one: marooning. I know a lovely little sandbar with a single palm for a bit of shade."

"Dare I be bold and ask what the second option may be?"

"If I am feeling generous, you'll meet the rope's end and take your chances on pleasing me." Fiona licked her lips and stroked the handle of her flogger. "If you please me, I may spare you the fate of the sandbar and make you part of my crew. That is if I am feeling generous. Or bored."

He squirmed on the bed. His cotton breeches left nothing to be imagined as his choice of punishments became clearly evident by the growing bulge drawing Fiona's eyes to his middle.

"I see you've chosen the second punishment, then?"

He nodded.

"Are you feeling bold?" she asked, standing up and swinging the cat slowly through the air next to her side.

"No, mi'lady. Nonetheless, I'd be foolish to turn down the opportunity to please a beautiful woman."

"I favor the bold and rarely suffer fools aboard the *Mi'Lady*. Remember, dead men tell no tales, William. So whatever shall occur here must not leave the cabin, let alone the ship."

"You have my word, mistress."

"The value of your word must be earned. Let's see how you deal with my favorite cat." With those words, she swung the flogger high above her head. The descent of the leather straps stirred the air of the cabin. The first contact caused him to close his eyes and cry out.

"Shhh. Silence. For each time you cry out, I shall add another stroke."

Her next few strikes moved across his chest, occasionally landing on his upper thighs, but she was always careful to avoid the prominent ridge at the top of his pants.

"Me thinks the gentleman is enjoying the pussy."

He had his eyes clenched tight and his hands fisted the ropes binding him to the bed, but did not respond.

"Wonderful. Your obedience is better than your word. You may speak, William."

"Thank you, mistress. While my chest is afire, my body feels awakened. Alive."

"I think we're off to a beautiful beginning," she said as she gently stroked the welts on his chest. Gliding her hand lower, she grasped him in her hand over the linen of his pants. Neither his length nor his girth was contained by her hand. "Oh, yes. We're off to a most beautiful beginning." With those words, she undid the laces of his pants and revealed his cock. Her mouth soon replaced her hand, laving him with her tongue before tasting the saltiness at the tip. She stretched her mouth around him, dragging her teeth along the underside of his cock before taking him fully in her mouth.

He bucked his hips but did not speak.

Standing upright, she commanded him, "Lift your hips," before pulling down the obstructive fabric of his pants. His legs were still splayed and tethered to the posts at the corners of her bed while his arms remained above his head.

Removing her own clothing, she mused over the man before her and in which position she would ride him. While his eyes were deep and soulful, she rarely faced her new conquests. Eye contact was to be earned for it was far too intimate. She toyed with herself, rubbing her clit and pushing a single finger inside. Using the flogger always aroused her beyond anything except a talented mouth.

Assuring herself he was still restrained, she stroked his length, spreading the moisture from the tip to create a slickness. She mounted him, facing away from the headboard. He stretched her far more than Robert. She rocked and moaned when her ass slowly settled against his hips.

"Do I please you, mi' lady?" he whispered.

"So far you do. I must say that you conceal the length of your sword very well. I had my suspicions, but am more than pleasantly surprised. Now, enough of this chatter. Let me see what you can do with your blade."

Her rocking alternated with bouncing as she rode him hard. Reaching up, she tweaked and pulled at her nipples. She stifled a moan by biting the inside of her cheek. Close to coming undone, she paused until she regained her control. No man had ever brought her to the edge so quickly. She would definitely be keeping him around.

Reaching the edge, she let herself fall. Her body spasmed as she continued rocking. When the last of the waves of pleasure ceased, she realized that he was still stiff inside her. His own pleasure not yet achieved. She looked at him over her shoulder.

"Have you held off your own release?"

With a strained, husky voice, he answered, "I have, mi' lady. My life depended on pleasing you, not seeking my own glory."

"Your life will be spared. At least for another day. You have more than pleased me." She leaned over him to release his legs, rubbing his ankles where the bindings made pink marks.

"Now that I've spared you from marooning, you must swear your loyalty to me and my ship to remain. Do you do so?" she asked as she rose from the bed to loosen the remaining bindings.

"I do, mi' lady. You have my word and my body as proof of my loyalty."

"You are a foolish man, William. You must realize you are in the company of a pirate captain." She released his arms. He stretched out his arms and rolled his neck.

With his shackles gone, he sat up before responding, "Aye, Captain Fiona."

William

Only the cries of gulls and the waves could be heard as William watched shock cross Fiona's face. Awaiting her answer, he gazed up at long tendrils of raven colored hair, eyes the color of the Sargasso Sea, and lips the color of a hibiscus bloom. Her skin was flushed from their encounter and her bosom heaved with her shocked breath.

He recalled how stunned he was to awake and see her sitting in only her white chemise and bloomers. The cat o'nine tails looked out of place in her delicate hand. Or perhaps it was the innocent white of her ensemble that was incongruous with the woman and her surroundings. He found himself spellbound by her beauty. She was indeed a rare gem.

His attention distracted by Fiona's beauty, he failed to notice her shift above him. When he felt his legs squeezed in a vice of her thighs, it was too late. Once again, he found himself on his back and at her mercy.

"Tsk, tsk, Mr. Boarder," she chided him. "If you plan to make a play to escape, you must keep your focus." To emphasize her point, she ground her hips on his torso, her heat seeping into his skin. His body responded. She laughed when she felt him begin to harden beneath her.

"I had no plans to escape, mi' lady. " He blinked innocently at her and rolled his hips.

"You called me Fiona, yet I do not have the memory of introducing myself other than as Captain."

"I must have heard one of your crew use the name, mi' lady."

Her stare told him she didn't believe his lie.

"No one calls me anything but captain outside of this cabin. No, that cannot be it."

He looked frantically around the dark wood paneled cabin for something to cover his error. Spying a small handkerchief on the dresser amongst the silver candelabra and assorted jewels, he sighed with relief. "Your handkerchief, Captain, is monogrammed with an F." He gestured to the scrap of embroidered linen. "I guessed. My second guess was Frances."

Fiona frowned at his explanation, glancing at the dresser. "I suspect you are lying. I don't know how you know my name, but you do. You are a liar and a snoop. Therefore, it is best to keep my eye on you. You're lucky you pleased me in bed, or I'd be tempted to keelhaul you and find out the truth. I'm sure the keel is covered with barnacles sharp enough to draw out both blood and the truth. Despite my suspicions about you, your timing is impeccable as I've grown bored of Fair Robert. And if your words are truth and not more lies, then I shouldn't be sharing my affections with him anymore, nor my trust. I shall keep you onboard the ship, but you will be my personal cabin boy."

With that she gave his torso a final squeeze with her thighs and dismounted. She eyed his erection and recalled that he hadn't yet come.

"I am pleased to be at your service, mi' lady. I shall not forget your kindness, and it will be my duty to please you at your command." He made no move to get off the bed, awaiting her instructions.

"Very well then, you may fetch my bath and my breakfast," she said, donning a robe of red silk. The red against her dark hair and pale skin made her appear much more the buccaneer of legend.

He gathered his clothes from the floor and made his exit. Once in the alleyway outside the captain's quarters, he paused to catch his breath. He couldn't let himself slip again if he was to complete his quest for the truth about the Pink Pearl. Based upon what he overheard in the Golden Parrot, his new lover could be the missing piece in solving the mystery that had haunted him since childhood.

Following the narrow passage that led to stairs going further below deck, he let his nose guide him to the galley. The sound of boisterous men's voices confirmed he had found the galley and mess when he pushed through the door.

"Ah, I see the captain has indeed found herself a new pet," a man with blonde hair and an arrogant expression said upon seeing William standing in the doorway. "I didn't think you had it in you. Figured we'd be making a detour to her favorite sandbar."

The other men gathered around the long, battered wood table laughed. An old man with a glass eye laughed with them, but then offered William a hello. "Never you mind Robert sitting there." The man gestured at the arrogant blond. William recognized him as the man he'd followed from the tavern. "What is your name, young man?"

"William. William Boarder," he answered.

"I'm Scully and this is the fine crew of the *Mi'Lady*. We're a motley bunch and we don't take to strangers easily. You don't look like a pirate, nor British Navy, and since you survived a morning with the captain, you'll probably fit in just fine. Mind if you keep out of Robert's way. He's the captain's favorite."

At the praise, Robert's chin tilted up and he stared at William. "Listen to Scully. You may be the new pet, but don't go thinking you're special. Most pets last a week, some only a night before walking the plank, but I've been aboard this ship for over a year. Learn to keep your mouth shut. Even better, keep your eyes shut, too. The likes of us don't favor snoops. Or spies."

The other crew nodded in agreement, all giving William the once over. Motley didn't begin to describe this crew. Besides Scully's glass eye, two other crew members wore eye patches, one had his shirt pinned up to the shoulder indicating a missing arm, and the rest of the lot were a mix of deep ebony skin tones, shabby beards, and a theater troupe's array of costumes. These were Fiona's crew members. He wondered who amongst them was worthy of her trust. His eyes wandered back to Robert, who was still staring him down.

Without breaking eye contact with Robert, he announced, "The captain requested her bath and breakfast. Instruct me how and where to fetch both, and I'll leave you to your meal."

"What a good little pet you are," Robert sneered. "Best to leave us men to the duties of the ship while you play maid."

William's retort left his mouth before he thought through the consequences. "I believe I was man enough to please the lady more than once this morning."

All except Robert chuckled at his declaration. Scully patted him on the back and handed him a tray. Ignoring Robert's scowl, Scully told him, "Here's the captain's meal. I'll send Tom with the hot water for her bath. She takes it on deck. Something about the fresh air and sun being good for her." Lowering his voice, he continued, "But I believe our captain is a bit of an exhibitionist, matey."

He could feel his body react to the idea of Fiona's naked flesh exposed to the sun and curious eyes of her crew. He nodded to Scully and bid his leave to the other men. As he exited the galley, he overheard Robert say, "I'll give him a week. I'm willing to bet a doubloon on it." Other voices joined in with their bets. Not a single bet was cast that William would last more than a fortnight.

He wouldn't need a fortnight to confirm his suspicions. He could sense that his hunt for the Pink Pearl was heating up. His time with the captain only strengthened his convictions.

The Pink Pearl was aboard the *Mi'Lady*.

CHAPTER 5

William

Fiona commanded William to keep her company while she bathed. Scully was correct in his assumption that the captain was an exhibitionist. She had him wash her back as well as shampoo her hair. She evidently had no qualms about William or any of her crew seeing her in all her naked glory as she stood from the bath and awaited her silk robe.

"The crew bathes once in a new moon, but should you choose to be more civilized, you can use whatever hot water remains after my bath," she offered him.

Glancing at the rose scented water in the copper tub, he decided to refuse her offer and declined with a shake of his head.

"Suit yourself. I'm going to dress and meet with Sebastien. You are free to explore the ship. But remember," she reached up and pressed against the bruise on his skull, "snoops get marooned. Best to stick to the deck and the crow's nest. That is, if you don't have a fear of heights."

He glanced far above the deck at the crow's nest and shook his head again. As a child aboard a much different type of ship, he had been braver. And his left arm had the break in it to remind him.

When he turned to reply to Fiona, he discovered she had disappeared. For the moment he was alone. Gulls swooped overhead and the bright sunlight bounced off of the Caribbean Sea. Small islands could be seen in the distance, but otherwise the ship was alone on the water. Peering around the deck, he noticed the usual piles of ropes, a few casks with their bungholes sealed tight with corks, carefully coiled rigging as well as a pair of small cannons on both the port and starboard sides of the deck. Heading aft, he spied more ammunition and a few swords at the ready. The *Mi'Lady* was prepared for a fight. The ship rolled with the waves and he attempted to find his balance as he adjusted to being at sea again. Fiona was right; he had not ventured further than the harbor in more than a year's time. Before that voyage from Jamaica to Port de Neuf, it had been ten years since his last time aboard a ship. He swore he'd never follow in his father's footsteps. Nor would he end up in Davy Jones' locker.

A loud cough snapped him from his memories and back to the deck of the *Mi'Lady*. Robert was standing in front of him, idly tossing a dagger from hand to hand. His blond hair was loose and wild. A dangerous glint was in his eye as he stared at William.

"Ah, I didn't see you there, Robert. My apologies for disrupting you." He moved to step around him, but Robert stuck out his dagger and blocked William's escape.

"For a spy, you are not very good at being aware of your surroundings," Robert sneered.

"Perhaps that is because I am not a spy. I'm a tavern cook, although not a very good one. Not that it matters when the rum is strong and the ale flows." His attempt at a laugh to lighten the mood was met with silence and another sneer.

"You don't look like the typical tavern cook. Nor do you sound like you're from Port de Neuf. Or the islands. I'd bet a piece of gold that you are not who or what you say."

William knew his cover was thin at best. He could disguise his accent fairly well to fool the locals, but his King's English couldn't fool a native speaker.

"'Tis true, Robert. I am English born, but I am not a spy for the Royal Navy."

Robert flipped his dagger, caught it, and pressed the tip to the center of William's chest. "I know you followed me to the dock. And for that reason, I think my conversation at the Golden Parrot was overheard as well. What do you know of the Pink Pearl, my friend? Englishman to Englishman, matey"

"I sense that you and I will never be mates even if we are both sons of England. To answer your question, I know nothing of the gem you speak of other than idle gossip, rumors, and false hopes of those who have drank in the tavern. Pink pearls, hidden treasures—the likes of these things hold no charms for a landlubber tavern cook like me. I leave the adventures to braver men and fools."

Robert laughed, but it was a cold, menacing laugh. "I have a blade pointed at your heart and you dare call me a fool? Oh, you are the fool." He pressed the blade harder against William's skin, but not to the point of breaking through.

He had had enough of Robert's bullying. He'd been in his fair share of brawls and sword fights in the tavern. He was not the brawniest of men, but his speed could disarm the best of swordsmen. He stepped into the blade, causing Robert to relax his arm. This gave him the room to feign to the left before dipping down to pick up one of the swords from the nearby stash. In a flash of movement, the dagger dropped to the deck and he held the sword to Robert's throat.

"I am no fool," he spat the words at Robert. "Nor am I a traitor. Does your captain know of your meeting and the leather pouch?"

"What's this? Double sword play without me?" Fiona's voice asked from somewhere behind him. She stood on the deck dressed in crimson and black, her waist cinched with a corset above her full skirts.

"Nay, my captain. You'll see that your new pet has his sword drawn on me, while mine lays at my side. Perhaps he should walk the plank. Or be fed to the sharks?"

"Now, now Robert. I've only begun to have my fun with sweet William. You know the rules of my ship. If there is going to be sword play, I should always be involved. No fair playing amongst yourselves. Where is the delight in that for me?"

William's eyes widened and his heartbeat quickened at the sexual innuendo of the captain's words. Surely her intentions weren't to have them both. At the same time. He wasn't interested in such things. Was he? Could he be? How far was he willing to go to stay aboard the ship and find out the truth of the pearl?

"Robert, look at his face. I've shocked him into being a mute," Fiona said, with laughter in her voice.

As he struggled to find his voice, he watched Fiona's face break into a huge grin and she shook her dark hair.

"You have nothing to fear, William. You seem to have the advantage over Robert. In both skill and the size of your blade." She glanced at the sword in his hand and down to the dagger on the deck, but he sensed she was speaking in metaphors again. He smirked and heard Robert grumble.

"I've thought myself average, so the lady's compliment delights me. I'm happy that I please you."

"You do. Very much. Now since you have put Robert in his place, my company for the evening has been determined. William, join me in my cabin for supper. Robert, you can eat with the rest of the crew in the mess."

He was thrilled to spend more time with Fiona, but knew better than to show his pleasure in front of Robert, who was proving to be a formidable adversary.

"But, mi' lady, I always dine with you—" Robert began to protest.

"Now, don't pout. Your lips are better served doing other things." She touched her finger to Robert's bottom lip before lightly patting him on the cheek in a dismissive gesture.

He could sense Robert bristling as he was summarily put in his place.

"As you wish, Captain. Enjoy your dinner," Robert said with a bow to Fiona, but his stare was chilling when he looked at William. "May the sun rise another day to greet your eyes." It was a thinly veiled threat.

He watched as Fiona glanced between the men before squaring her shoulders. "The same to you, Robert. Tell Scully I'll be in my quarters with William until supper. No one is to bother me unless war ships are spotted or we encounter a storm." She turned and began to head down the stairs to her quarters.

"Come, William," she said without turning back.

Under his breath, Robert whispered, "Remember that the dead tell no tales, Mr. Boarder. Your time aboard this ship is limited."

Ignoring Robert's threat, he followed Fiona to her cabin.

He found her standing at her desk, idly toying with a small compass.

"What have you done to anger Robert? He has never hated someone new as quickly as he has with you. You were discovered following him down to the docks. Prove your loyalty to me and tell me the truth of that night. If you lie, I will know it."

He took a deep breath and held it for a moment. His fate would be sealed with his words. If he lied, she'd probably kill him. If he told her the truth, she could think it was a lie and kill him. Either way, he was facing the plank. Or worse.

CHAPTER 6

William

William swallowed. "Your Fair Robert met with an officer of the British Navy in the Golden Parrot," he spoke clearly, hoping she would hear the truth in his words.

"Ah, yes." She nodded. "I knew he was up to something after he insisted we stop in Port de Neuf again so soon after my encounter with the Royal Navy last month. Sebastien and Jack were sent ashore to keep an eye on him, but he lost them in an alley."

"I saw him enter the tavern through the kitchen. He passed by me and caught my eye. It isn't every day a buccaneer is in my kitchen."

"Why didn't you tell me this detail when questioned this morning? Does your loyalty lie with Robert or with me?" she asked, setting the compass down on the desk and walking over to her dresser. She picked up a silver comb and used it to pull up her hair, exposing her neck. There at the hairline was a small, round, pink birthmark. No bigger than a large pearl.

He choked on his breath and coughed before speaking.

"My loyalty is with you, Captain. Only you. I did not know

what favor Robert held with you. I was biding my time to discover his standing with you."

"And what have you discovered?" She turned to look at him.

"The truth?"

"Only the truth."

"He is not to be trusted. I think he has given the Navy information about the Pink Pearl. He seeks his own fortune above all things, mi' lady."

"Why should I believe you? Who are you to me that I should listen to your words above Robert's? He's been loyal to me and my pleasure for over a year." She cocked her head and stared at him.

"Because I know the secret of the Pink Pearl and why the Admiral Lindsley wants to find it so desperately. I believe Robert has figured out the mystery as well."

He heard her sharp intake of breath and watched as she reflexively brought her hand up to the back of her neck.

"You are the legendary Pink Pearl, Fiona Lindsley, lost niece of Rear Admiral Lindsley. The most valuable gem of the Caribbean. The treasure lesser men have sought and failed to find, despite it being right in front of their faces."

In a heartbeat, he felt the coldness of a blade of steel against his neck. He hadn't even seen her reach for her sword.

"You must be addled, Mr. Boarder. A pirate such as me has nothing to do with the Rear Admiral Lindsley."

"Nay, mi' lady. It's not bilgewater. The fair Miss Lindsley had a small birthmark on her neck. You bear the same one. I had my suspicions when I awoke in your quarters, but it wasn't until you pulled up your hair just now that everything was confirmed. The Rear Admiral seeks not his fortune, but his lost niece. You."

Fiona held the blade in place, but did not speak.

"Mi' lady?"

She stared at him, her eyes searching his face for a few moments before she spoke, "I know you. Your face was familiar to me. I assumed it was similar to those illustrations of English boys in children's books. I've tried to recall meeting someone named Boarder prior, but cannot."

He slowly walked over and sat beside her on the bed. "You won't recall a William Boarder. Boarder was not the name I was born with. Perchance you recall a Mountwell? Will Mountwell?"

At the sound of his real name, her sword clattered to the floor.

"Mountwell? Will? Of Jamaica Mountwells?" Her voice belayed her shock. Gone was all pretense of pirate cunning. All that remained was the beautiful girl he remembered.

"Yes, Fiona. I'm Will." He bowed and then laughed. "I believed you dead for many years."

"Yet you are standing here, in front of me, aboard my ship, holding my secrets. How did this come to pass?"

"It was the legend of the Pink Pearl, mi' lady. I knew your uncle would not seek treasure of gold and gems for he never put value in such things. I got wind of a pirate captain with hair the color of night and eyes that matched the Sargasso Sea. Legend of her beauty, mystery, and ability to elude the Navy were second only to the legends of the pearl that the Admiral sought to find. I took the cook's job at the Golden Parrot in hopes of crossing paths with you or your crew."

"Will Mountwell. The first boy I ever kissed. And the last." She gaped at him in awe.

"The last? But Mi' lady, Fiona, you couldn't mean that. Robert made it clear, as did you, that you take lovers at your will, tossing them aside for the next. Surely you have kissed others."

"I have not. Not even Robert. Sex is one thing. Matters of the heart and kissing are to be avoided in the life of a pirate."

He was stunned with her declaration. The great pirate captain had not kissed a man in ten years.

"Mi' lady—"

"Please, Will, call me Fiona. Heaven is my name falling from your lips."

"Fiona, I'm going to kiss you now."

Before she could answer, he grabbed her, bent her back, and kissed her. No fumbling school boy, no hesitations. He kissed her thoroughly until they were breathless. She tasted of salt and something sweet, like a rare chocolate.

"There is no treachery nor treason greater than letting these lips go unkissed for a moment longer."

Her bee-stung lips were swollen from their kiss, their color deepened to a garnet red. As she merely blinked back at him, he thought her never more beautiful. She should be thoroughly kissed. And often.

"Will?" she asked.

"Yes?"

"Fuck me. Now. Please."

Wil laughed. "Since you said please, how could I say no?"

Stripping off her garments, he reveled in her naked flesh. Slowly, he tortured her with his hands, gliding over her skin with the lightest of touches as if she was the most fragile piece of glass. He picked her up and then tossed her on the bed. She sighed and writhed beneath him.

"Please," she murmured.

Feeling heady with his power over her, he smiled and bit her hip, leaving a small mark where he sucked on her flesh.

"Ow!" Fiona shouted and swiftly reversed their positions on the bed. She held his arms above his head in her hands, her thighs clamped tight around his hips. Glowering down at him, she growled. "Lest you get the wrong idea, I am still the captain. And still a pirate. Not a school girl who swoons over boys."

"Aye, aye," he said, grinning up at her. Her fiery nature thrilled him, but he wasn't about to give in to her power trip. As quickly as he had found himself on his back, he flipped her over and pinned her with his body. "Lest ye get the wrong idea, I'm a man, not a schoolboy." He thrust his hips into hers to emphasize his point. "And this is a sword, not a dagger, mi'lady. I've heard your sword skills are legendary. Let's see what you can do with mine."

She bit his lip when he bent to kiss her, but he didn't let that stop his advance. His tongue found hers and her moan told him that as much as she protested, his actions pleased her.

Reaching between them, she undid his pants and claimed him with her hands. When she squeezed him, his moan was one of both pleasure and pain.

He desired to dominate her, to claim her as his. No man would share her bed again if he had his way.

He removed her hand and stroked himself. He was hard as marble. Reaching between her thighs, he plunged two fingers into the moisture he found there and used it on his cock. She watched him stroke his length, her hips undulating in a silent plea.

"You asked to be fucked," he said, meeting her eyes before thrusting into her warmth. "And so you shall be." He thrust again, harder and deeper. Her eyes rolled back into her head, but she made no move to take control.

With each thrust, he rocked deep within her. He could feel his entire cock wrapped in her wet heat. He needed more, so he lifted her legs, placing them on his shoulders. The new angle allowed him to lean forward so his pelvis hit the spot that made her moan louder.

"More," she whispered. "More."

Wanting to please her, he reached between their bodies to find the secret hidden below her curls. The pearl found there was the reward he sought.

He felt Fiona clench and spasm around him, her back arching off the bed.

Let the fools and addled seek gems and gold. Wise men knew that a woman's pleasure was the rarest treasure.

Fiona opened her eyes and smiled at him. "Come for me."

"As you wish, mi' lady," he replied. Unable to hold back any longer, he thrust into her twice more before tremoring and filling her. Resting his head on her bosom, he panted, trying to catch his breath.

Her hand came up to stroke his hair and he turned to face her. He couldn't resist seizing the opportunity to kiss her again and he leaned toward her.

Loud knocks on the cabin's door stopped him before their lips could meet.

"Captain?" Scully's voice carried through the thick wood of the door.

"Scully, I told you to only interrupt me if we were being pursued."

"Aye, Captain. We are."

CHAPTER 7

Fiona

Fiona reacted to Scully's words by shoving Will out of the way and leaping out of the bed.

"Who is in pursuit?" she asked, donning whatever clothing lay on the floor. She tossed Will's shirt over her head and tied it with the sash of silk from her robe; it would have to do. There was no time for corsets and pantaloons.

"A warship of the Royal Navy, Captain," Scully answered.

Fiona's eyes widened. "Get dressed. You don't want to be caught without your pants when the Royal Navy is involved."

"Has Robert prepared the cannon if needed?" Fiona asked.

"No, Mistress. Fair Robert cannot be found."

Fiona flung open the door to find Scully standing there, wringing his hands.

"Well, why the hell not? Is he sleeping?"

"Nay, the ship's been searched. As soon as the Union Jack was spotted, the call went out for Robert. He's gone. The skiff's gone, too. He's abandoned ship, mi' lady."

"That bilgewater, barnacled cock, scurvied bastard," Fiona swore as she shoved past Scully with Will in her wake.

Ships could be seen in the distance when they reached the deck. Sebastien was at the helm and the sails were unfurled. The *Mi'Lady* had size and speed on her side, but the Navy had the numbers and weaponry on theirs.

"Bloody hell. If I ever lay eyes upon Fair Robert again, it will be my pleasure to cut off his jewels. Filthy traitor. Shark bait is too good for him."

She took the helm from Sebastien and ordered the crew to prepare. "If we can get ahead of them, we can find safe harbor in Turtle Cove. We've been spotted, but they don't know anything more than we're a ship without the King's flag."

Will approached her, looking nervous. "How can I be of service, Captain?"

She smiled at him. "Are you ready for the pirate life, Mr. Mountwell?"

"I'll go wherever you go, Fiona." He bowed his head before lowering his lips and kissing her.

Rowdy cheers burst from the crew.

Fiona broke the kiss and gave the crew a stern warning with her eyes. "Aye, yes, I've been kissed. Anyone who mentions it again, shall be the first to walk the plank. Are we clear?"

The crew nodded and murmured, "Yes, Captain," behind smiles.

"Right then, let's focus. We have a Royal Navy to outrun." She turned and shouted orders to the crew to open the sails as she took the helm. "Let's show those fools that no warship will overtake the *Mi'Lady*. All hands on deck!"

The wind was in their favor as they soon put a knot, then two, between them and the masts of the warship. The pirate ship was smaller and easily maneuvered to take advantage of the winds. Calm seas and cloud cover aided their escape as the *Mi'Lady* cut silently through the waves.

"Land ho!" called One Eyed Jack from his perch in the crow's nest.

Fiona peered through the indigo night, which was quickly turning to violet with the approaching dawn, to see the faint outline of a small island that was home to one of her hiding places. A sheltered cove invisible to the unfamiliar eye would provide them safe port for the time.

As the *Mi'Lady* sailed into Turtle Cove and the sun hit the sails, they turned a pale pink. The Pink Pearl had escaped capture once again. Nevertheless Fiona knew that Fair Robert was out there somewhere, biding his time and his secrets to the highest offer. Now that she had Will by her side again, she felt invincible, but how much longer could she sail the high seas foiling her uncle's quest to find her and bring her back to England?

I've always planned to continue these adventures on the high seas. No set date to write or publish more pirotica, but never say never.

Modern Love Stories:
We Were Here (prequel to Geoducks)
Geoducks Are for Lovers
Wanderlust
Happily Ever Now (coming late 2017)

Wingmen:
Ready to Fall
Confessions of a Reformed Tom Cat
Anything but Love
Better Love
Small Town Scandal (coming June 2017)

Love with Altitude:
Next to You
Crazy Over You
Wild for You (coming later in 2017)
Up to You (2018)

Bewitched
A magical short set in Salem, Massachusetts
Spellbound
A magical sequel to Bewitched
Enchanted
A magical continuation (coming September 2017)

aisy Prescott is a USA Today bestselling author of contemporary romantic comedies, including Modern Love Stories, the Wingmen series, and the Love with Altitude series.

Daisy currently lives in a real life Stars Hollow in the Boston suburbs with her husband, their rescue dog Mulder, and an indeterminate number of imaginary house goats. When not writing, she can be found in the garden or kitchen, lost in a good book, or on social media, usually talking about hot, bearded men and sloths.

Make sure you're subscribed to my monthly emails. I share exclusive shorts, sneak peeks, excerpts, and all my latest news directly to your inbox. I promise never to spam you. You can subscribe at www.daisyprescott.com/newsletter/

To learn more about Daisy and her writing visit:
www.daisyprescott.com

Or find her on social media:
Twitter: @daisy_prescott
Facebook: www.facebook.com/DaisyPrescottAuthor
Pinterest: www.pinterest.com/daisyprescott/
Instagram: daisyprescott